The Edge of Mysterion

Another Tale of Mysterion

by
Richard René

CONCILIAR
PRESS
CHESTERTON, INDIANA

The Edge of Mysterion
Copyright © 2011 Richard René

Published by Conciliar Press
A division of Conciliar Media Ministries
P.O. Box 748
Chesterton, IN 46304

Printed in the United States of America

ISBN 10: 1-936270-34-X
ISBN 13: 978-1-936270-34-7

Cover art by Gary Lippincott (www.garylippincott.com)
Map on p. 7 by Isabelle René

Library of Congress Cataloging-in-Publication Data

René, Richard, 1974-
The edge of Mysterion : another tale of Mysterion / by Richard René.
   p. cm. -- (The Mysterion ; bk. 2)
Summary: Running away from a violent father and a broken home, teenaged
Isabella finds herself in Mysterion, a hidden world peopled by Cyclops and
giant turtles, dragons and mermaids, and winged Angeli.

ISBN 978-1-936270-34-7
[1. Fantasy.] I. Title. II. Series.

PZ7.R2852Ed 2011
[Fic]--dc23

2011029608

To my beloved Jaime, of course
And to the sad girl who inspired Isabella

A NOTE ON THE
WORLD OF MYSTERION

Welcome to Mysterion. For those of you who have been here before, you need not pause. Move on, if you wish, to the adventure that follows. For you who reside in Lethes and have never entered this world, allow me, your faithful narrator and guide, to offer you a little guidance as you begin this new journey.

Mysterion is not a place you can find on a map. However far and fast you travel, by land or sea or air, you will never arrive. And yet you will always be there, for Mysterion is wherever you are and somewhere else, all at once.

Of Mysterion's history you will learn in the story to come: how the Wind made a space in which the world could breathe; how the people of the Wind dwelt together with the creatures we now know only in dreams and visions; how they were soon divided from one another—heart against mind, body against soul—until two worlds came to be: Lethes, the world of forgetfulness, and Mysterion, the world forgotten.

Letheis like you and me, who dwell in a world without memory, can no longer see the glorious expanse of Mysterion. It has been hidden from our sight within the stream of infinitesimal moments that flows through our lives. Only during those times when something is broken or lost can we possibly find our way back. Only when our world is no longer as it should be can we discover the world as it once was and always has been.

A long time ago, while sailing from India to the port of Zanzibar, a man named Acquille was sacrificed by his shipmates to appease the Djinn of a storm. As he drowned, he found himself in Mysterion, the first of the Letheis to return since the time of separation. There he was given a Lamp—the work of the many-winged Angeli who watch over and protect Mysterion from its enemies. With this Lamp, he was told he might guide others back to the world to which they had become blind.

Returning to his life, Acquille learned to kindle the Lamp, and then found an apprentice to whom he could teach this art. This young man, named Francis, found the labor of the Lamp too much, however, and soon abandoned his effort. Acquille found himself alone, a hermit surrounded by books, the Lamp gathering dust in a corner.

Many years later, Francis Comfait disappeared. Believing he had been swept off his ship during a storm, the people of Anse Aux Pins—the little island community where he lived—mourned him. Only his son Jonah refused to believe that Francis was dead. Unable to imagine a world in which his father did not exist, Jonah soon began a quest to find him, a quest that led him to Acquille and into Mysterion. I will say no more of his adventures there; you may read more about them in *The Nightmare Tree*, the first tale of Mysterion. All I will say now is that Jonah came back to his life here in Lethes, where he took up Acquille's task of teaching the secrets of the Lamp to one for whom the world was not as it should be.

And yet, even as he returned to Lethes, Jonah lived on in Mysterion, where he cared for the people of the Wind. Such is the paradox of Mysterion, which you would do well to keep in mind as you go forward on this journey. For our time in Mysterion is always and only a single moment in the world of forgetfulness. My tale is told in the forgetful world you know. Therefore, my words can be no more than an imperfect image of the real story being told both here and elsewhere, both now and always. The best I can offer is a crudely fashioned replica of the Lamp that reveals things as they truly are. I hope it is sufficient for now.

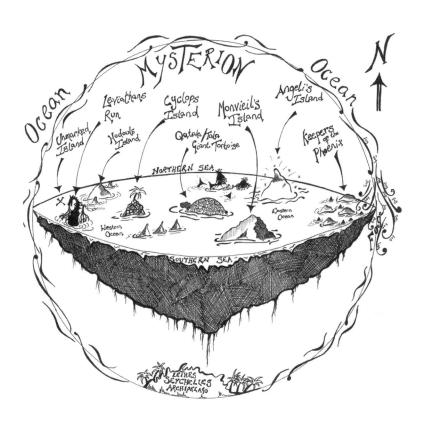

Editor's Note: French and other unfamiliar words and phrases are marked with an asterisk (*) and defined in the Glossary on page 215.

LETHES I

Isabella Morgan ran in the darkness. Overhead the wind whipped the trees around in a frenzy. Far behind her she could still hear her father shouting, "She cut me, the little vixen cut me!"— fading as she pressed deeper into the forest. The undergrowth clung to her and the night heat thickened to the consistency of old oil, resisting her. But she struggled on, blind with the tears that rose in sobs.

At last, the trees opened into a small clearing flooded with moonlight. Scattered around the clearing, gravestones, overgrown with moss and lichen and vines, lay in a rough arrangement of rows. Some leaned at odd angles or sank into decay, their inscriptions almost indecipherable. Others stood straight and clean-cut against the assaults of time and decrepitude.

Isabella had discovered the cemetery three years earlier, after a similar incident with her parents. She had come here so many times since that she could find it even when an internal hurricane was tearing her apart, as it was again tonight.

Seized by fits of crying and with her head bowed, she stumbled to her favorite spot at the far corner of the cemetery, where the trees cast impenetrable shadows. The stone there was the largest of the markers, a granite slab worn and rounded with age, grey with lichen and leaning back slightly. Isabella had cut back the growth around the grave to make room. Now she collapsed against the stone, drawing up her knees to her face and closing her eyes against her tears.

Papa had come home drunk, as always. He and Maman had gone at each other about the usual suspects: his unemployment (*"All you can do is play with cars that never get fixed and get drunk with your friends at the roadside, and whistle at every skirt you see!"*); Maman's parentage (*"Your mother was in every bed on Mahe except the bishop's! You are not sure to this day who your father really is!"*); and finally, their favorite source of complaint: Isabella. (*"A fat lot of good the NYS* did for her! Half her friends come out pregnant, and she worse than ever, her and that thirty-year-old man, Maxim whatever-he-is, smoking marijuana down at the beach!"*)

Maxim was what really set her father off.

Isabella's sobs faded, leaving something dull and empty in their place. This feeling had once disturbed her, but now it came as a relief, almost pleasant. Above, the moon sailed out from behind a cloud. As if disturbed by her recollections, the wind rattled the branches. Clouds drew a curtain over the moon.

Isabella felt a presence nearby. She looked around.

A man had appeared in the middle of the cemetery. Isabella could not guess his age; his face could have belonged to any number of people she had met and forgotten—short curly hair, slender build, indistinct jawline. Only his clothes—full suit and tie—and the extreme pallor of his complexion struck her as unusual.

Stepping among the stones, he sat down in front of her, cross-legged. She felt no fear. She was used to sitting by the sea road, talking to anyone who happened by. Besides, there was nothing particularly disconcerting about this young man, other than a curious deadness in his eyes.

"You look comfortable, Mam'zelle," the young man said. "Settling in?" A grin spread over his lips without touching his eyes.

"I like it here," Isabella said.

"Well, at least the dead don't natter your ear off," the man agreed.

"I heard a story once of a woman who brought all the news to her husband's grave. Told him about this and that, you know. And what did she get for her troubles? He came back as a poltergeist and tore up her house. Apparently he was upset Rose had sold all his things after he died."

The young man chuckled and shook his head.

"I've heard all the stories," Isabella said. "I don't remember that one."

The young man looked at her quizzically. "It happened a long time ago. Long before you were born, when people still believed in poltergeists. No doubt things like that don't happen these days."

"Still," Isabella insisted. "I would know it. I talk to the old-timers."

"Yes." The young man nodded. "I know you do."

Isabella's eyes narrowed. "What do you mean?"

"I've watched you."

She straightened up. "I've never seen you. Who are you, anyway?"

The young man looked mortified. "Did I forget to introduce myself?" He slapped his face. "Bad, bad boy! Well, it's never too late, is it? My name is Malach. Pleased to meet you, Isabella Morgan!"

Isabella regarded the pale, soft-looking hand Malach held out to her.

"I don't know that name," she said.

"Probably not," Malach said. "But you *have* seen me. You just forgot my face. It is rather forgettable, isn't it? Or," he continued, inspired by an afterthought, "perhaps you did not recognize me."

"Why wouldn't I recognize you?" Isabella asked, thinking: *Perhaps he escaped from St. Claire's madhouse.*

Malach shrugged. "Sometimes we are not who we seem. Won't you shake?"

Isabella shook her head. "I don't shake hands with strangers. Especially not in cemeteries at midnight."

"But it's morning already!" Malach cried, gesturing widely at the sky, where the moon had sunk out of sight and the air had lost its impenetrable quality, acquiring a dimension of blue. "And besides, how would you make friends if you did not first shake the hand of a stranger?"

"You want to be my friend?"

"Absolutely," Malach declared, stretching his hand further towards her.

"Why?"

"Do friends need a reason to be friends, other than mutual affection?"

"Perhaps I don't want your affection."

Malach raised his eyebrows. "Why not?"

Isabella's smile was twisted. "Are you mad? You're a stranger approaching me in a cemetery!"

Comprehension dawned on Malach's face. "Oh, for goodness' sake, my dear girl . . . No, no, no! A creature like me does not require such base pleasures! If you only knew . . . No." He grew serious. "I seek only your welfare. Your freedom, Isabella. Now, come on. Shake, and I will tell all!"

"Fine," Isabella said. "I don't care anyway." Cursorily, she reached out. Malach grabbed her hand.

At once, he seemed to explode. His skin darkened. Muscles bulged and coiled in his arms as his suit ripped and vanished. His head stretched into a long, angular shape, like the skull of an ox, while horns spread out above his ears. Wings sprouted from behind his shoulders, reminding Isabella of the illustrations of pterodactyls she had seen in her science textbook.

"Oh, silly me!" he cried, once the transformation was complete. "I seem to have lost my disguise."

Isabella had scrambled around behind the grave marker, her heart throwing itself against her ribcage.

"Surprised?" Malach said.

"What are you?" Isabella shouted.

"Have you ever heard of a genie?"

Isabella said nothing.

"Three wishes? Yes?"

"You . . . you're a genie?"

"An insult to my kind!" Malach shouted. "No, I am not a genie! I am a Djinn of the tribe of Shaitan!"

"Then why did you disguise yourself?"

"It is necessary to do so for the comfort of weak-minded humans. But in your case, I made an exception."

"Where do you come from?"

"A faraway place. A place you can only imagine." He paused, and then added harshly, "*Can* you imagine such a place? Or is this your idea of paradise?" The air had taken on the translucent quality of early dawn. The dampness of dew coated Isabella's skin, making her shiver.

"Why are you here?" Malach demanded. "Do you not like your home?"

"No." Isabella's voice shook. "I hate it." *Three wishes . . .*

Malach's eyes glowed like coals in the semi-darkness. "Why?"

Her father's feet slapped down the hallway towards her room. He tried the door handle, then pounded.

"Open this door!" he shouted.

"You stay out of here!" she yelled. She was trembling now.

"Didn't I tell you to stay away from Maxim?"

"He's my friend! What do you care?"

"I told you to stay away from him. He's a shady character!"

"It's none of your business!"

"None of my business? I'll give you none of my business. Open this door or I will break it down, I tell you!"

Rummaging in the bureau among her underwear, she found her switchblade and flicked it open. "You don't go crazy," Max had said, when he entrusted it to her. "But when they come at you, you have to take care of things." He whipped it around as he had seen Bruce Lee do in Fists of Fury.

Isabella spoke at last: "Because my papa is a pig and my maman is a cow."

Malach's eyebrows rose. "Strong words! And what exactly have they done to deserve such condemnation?"

Isabella folded her arms and looked away.

"They get drunk, don't they?"

Isabella looked at him. "If you knew, why did you ask?"

"Because I wanted *you* to tell me." Malach jabbed a claw-like finger at her face. "So they get a little soused! What's so wrong with drowning your sorrows in *calou** once in a while? After all—"

"That's not all they do."

"Then what?"

Isabella was silent. The memories of the evening were strong upon her.

"Isabella!" her father bellowed.

"Isabella, open the door, baby," her mother bleated. "He's going to kick it!"

"Now you'll see!" her father said. With a loud bang, he kicked at the door. It cracked and shivered but just held. Isabella heard him grunt. Then he hit again, and the door exploded inward. They way he strode in towards her, with that look on his face, she knew she would be sobbing in the corner when he was done. He wouldn't break anything, but the bruises would last.

"When my father gets drunk—" Tears filled Isabella's eyes and she stopped. "He hurts me," she managed at last.

Malach's words were laced with a measure of pity. "And your mother?"

Her mother . . . Maman appeared in the doorway now and saw Isabella pointing the switchblade at her father. She clapped her hands over her mouth and cried, "Oh my Jesus, Joseph and Mary!"

"Stay away from me," Isabella told her father. Then glancing at her mother, "Both of you leave me alone!"

"Give that to me." His voice sounded strangled.

"No."

"Give it to me!" He lunged forward. Isabella ducked and stabbed upward in the same motion. Her father yelled and stumbled sideways, collapsing on her bed. Isabella found herself still holding the knife, dark, sticky blood coating the blade and her hand. Maman rushed forward and collapsed by the bed. "Ray, mon pauvre*, look what she did to you!" Then she raised her face to Isabella and spat, "Are you happy now? You killed your own father!"

"She doesn't care," Isabella sniffed. "She just sits there staring in front of her and smoking a cigarette. And when she's sober and I tell her what happened, she just looks at me like I'm touched."

"Why don't you run away?"

"What do you think I'm doing here?"

"But why don't you stay away?"

"Where would I go?" Isabella shouted. "Everyone on this stinking island knows me or my parents! I can't go to Praslin because my papa's family is from there and they'd send me back. I can't go to my auntie on La Digue—she's such a religious type I couldn't stand her—" As she spoke, Isabella pulled the medallion out, sliding it back and forth on its leather cord.

Malach leaned forward with interest.

"I am sorry to interrupt," he said. "But what is that stunning piece of jewelry?"

Isabella paused and looked down at the medallion.

"My papa gave me that," she said. "When I was little. It's a doubloon. He got it from his father, who got it from his father, all the way back. He said our ancestor was hanged as a pirate, and this was part of a great treasure that was lost a long time ago. Our ancestor kept a piece as proof."

"Is that what you talk to the old-timers about?" Malach asked. "To find out clues to the hidden treasure?"

Isabella shrugged.

"Well, I must say it's a precious gift," Malach murmured thoughtfully. "It reminds me of another I saw once . . ." He broke off. "A precious gift from someone who truly cares about you."

"He gave it to me a long time ago," Isabella said. "He was different then."

"So you keep on going back. Because of a single good memory?"

"I said I have nowhere else to go. Besides, it's none of your damn business!"

"But if you could go somewhere else, you would."

"Of course! I'd leave that hole in a heartbeat!"

"Then," Malach said with an arch smile, "why not go somewhere far away, where no one will recognize you?"

"Leave the islands? I can't afford—"

"No, that's not what I mean." Malach paused for emphasis. "I mean go to the place I can show you."

The trees were alive with birds. The sky had paled to the color of roses. The grasses bowed under the dew.

Malach continued softly. "Imagine a place far away from this suffering. Nobody would know you because no one there remembers this world. They have all forgotten about their miserable lives in this hell, and found what they were looking for. They are finally free, you understand? You could get lost and never get found. You could even give yourself a new name." He was looking at her closely now.

Isabella half sniffed, half laughed. Malach grinned and spread his arms. "I don't know—whatever you want!"

"Is that one of the wishes you grant?" Isabella asked mockingly. "A new name?"

Malach's grin faded into a cold smile as he shook his head. "I've told you—I don't grant wishes like some fairy-tale creature. I am telling you of Mysterion because I see that you are suffering at the hands of those who should love you. But there is a cost to enter. And that, I'm afraid, is something I cannot waive merely because I happen to like you."

Isabella looked suspicious. "So there is a price."

"Of course," Malach replied. "Everything comes with a price, even friendship—though that is somewhat less tangible than this . . ." He reached out and opened his hand. Something heavy dropped and dangled at the end of an iron chain. A stone that resembled a piece of charcoal. As she looked, it somehow got blacker and more impenetrable, as if it were feeding on her vision.

"When you take the enchanted stone, you will purchase a Chant that I, the vendor, will pronounce on your behalf, gaining you access to Mysterion forever." Malach's voice had turned dry, like a lawyer reading from a legal document. "In taking the stone, you bind yourself to the condition of purchase, which is service to the Djinn as payment for your entrance. You will serve us until payment is made in full, at which time you will be free to live in Mysterion until death."

Isabella was silent. She could not believe she was listening to this creature and his insanity of magical stones and imaginary places. And yet here he was before her, holding something truly fascinating.

"How will I," she found herself saying, "how will I serve you?"

"Nothing too onerous," Malach said. "Believe me, you'll practically sleep your way through it—ha-ha."

"But what is it?"

"I cannot explain it here. You must come and see in order to understand."

"But supposing I see and I don't want to do it?"

"Then it will be too late, I'm afraid."

Streaks of sunlight now pushed through the trees. She noticed Malach wince and shrink deeper into the shade.

"Don't like the sunlight?" she asked.

"I sunburn easily." Malach's smile was a grimace. "Besides, I cannot be seen in my civvies, so to speak. Which is why I will be leaving in a less than a minute, with or without you."

Isabella shook her head. "I don't know . . ."

"What do you have to lose? This little cemetery where you come before your time, like little old Rose who couldn't live in reality once she lost her old man? Or perhaps you will miss your parents?"

A wave of indifference swept suddenly over Isabella. Servitude, or this—what did it matter, anyway? Closing her eyes, she reached out and clutched the stone dangling from the Djinn's hand.

Several things happened at once. Malach began to chant in a strange language that seemed to be made only of consonants. Daylight retreated from the cemetery, light sucked back into the East. Darkness rose overhead, and at the same time, with a silent rush, a tide of black water swelled and poured out of the trees, flooding the clearing, drowning the graves. It rose up cold around her and swirled around her waist, her chest. Isabella scrambled to her feet, but the black water reached her neck even as she stood up. Malach had vanished in the confusion, and now the freezing water rose over her head. She flailed, tried to pull her way to the surface, but there was no surface to find. Her lungs heaved, and black liquid filled her mouth.

Then iron-hard claws were dragging her up and out as she coughed up the bitter water. It was night again, and she lay on a patch of white sand in the moonlight. The air stank of pig's excrement.

A voice like nails on a blackboard spoke: "Lift her!"

Upright and hanging from the claws of two creatures who resembled Malach, she looked around her blearily. At the edge of the clearing, a forest reached up skeletal hands, and a host of Djinn hissed and flapped their wings in the bare branches. Before her stood a bloated, alien-looking baobab tree.

A Djinn with a pale, lifeless face stood beside the tree. He was taller than the rest and wore a tattered cloak.

"Bring her forward!" the Djinn screamed. His eyes were empty holes.

"Welcome to your new home, Isabella Morgan."

He dug his claws into the baobab's trunk and pulled an opening apart. Then, reaching into his cloak, he brought out a collar of some dull, heavy metal, hinged on one side. Before Isabella could struggle, he slipped the circle of metal around her neck and clicked it shut. At once, the world drained of its color. A wave of nausea swept over her. The Djinn's voice came from far away:

"I am Lord Geist. I look forward to observing your suffering. Put her in!"

Isabella felt herself dragged forward. Then she was falling in darkness that stank of sweat and excrement. She hit the ground on her side, and found herself lying in her room at home, curled in a fetal position. The night's heat was a solid thing pressing down, with only the space under the door for light. The sharp coir fiber of her mattress mingled with the sweat-stink of a sheet that hadn't been washed in who-knows-when. And her parents' shouting came at her again from under the door.

CHAPTER ONE

BELLA GETS AWAY

Bella Couteau ran in the darkness. The wind roared overhead, keeping pace with her in the trees and muting the slap of her feet on the beaten path. A hundred yards behind came the shouts of her pursuer.

He's definitely falling behind. Not yet, though. She needed to gain at least fifty yards before she could risk turning off. Slapping at her pocket to make sure her prize was still there, she leaned into her run.

The path angled uphill. The coconut trees retreated; thicker vegetation closed around her and met overhead, blocking out the sky. The air enclosed her like a damp hand, and fresh rivulets of sweat ran into her eyes. Bella swept a hand over her face and leapt up along the path, trusting instinct and memory to guide her. She could no longer hear him. Now was safe, she decided, and turned aside, pushing several yards into the bushes before squatting into stillness.

The sound of panting reached her. A light swelled from the direction of the path—Joe Granbousse's lamp; then a gurgling, as if Joe were inhaling water, and his voice, high and petulant:

"Damned—bloody thief—I'll be seeing you marooned with the Cyclops by evening. I'll be watching the monster use your guts to clean the flesh from his teeth, by the Tyrant—I'll be laughing . . ."

Bella grinned to imagine the pear-shaped merchant with the flaps of loose skin under his arms quivering and dripping. For as long as she had been with the Brethren, he had never joined in a raid. This fact alone made him a pleasure to despise. A leech like that could hardly claim the rights of faithful men. He deserved to be stolen from. He practically *begged* for it.

"Yes, sir, absolutely correct sir," came a second voice, breathless and squeaky. Bella chuckled and rolled her eyes. Wherever Joe Granbousse went, Apoojamy was sure to follow, circling like a fruit fly while his head bobbed continually. He was as thin as Joe was fat, reaching as high as the merchant's chest. Constantly in motion, Apoojamy's limbs jerked and shifted even when he sat, but no matter how slowly his master moved, he always seemed to lag behind.

"We'll both be laughing, sir," Apoojamy continued. "That is an absolute guarantee. I saw the fellow well, sir, quite well. I am almost absolutely one hundred percent certain I could spot the rogue . . ."

Bella covered her mouth to stop the laughter. Apoojamy had seen her, all right—seen her so clearly he thought she was a *boy* . . . Well, good! When Apoojamy had descended the stairs into the merchant's cellar and discovered her crawling back up the hatchway whose lock she had picked, he started shouting, "Stop thief! Stop, despicable delinquent!" And then, calling up the stairs to the merchant, "Come, sir, come!" She had not known until now whether or not he had identified the shape of her body.

Clearly not, the arse-kisser.

"Let them be lined up," he was squeaking. "And I shall certainly identify him, almost absolutely I shall."

"And well you may, Apoojamy," Joe Granbousse replied. "Well you may. For I will not be letting this rest, of that you can be assured, Apoojamy. It was two pounds of my best Dragon's claw powder! Do you realize the labor of acquiring such a quantity? Not to be taken lightly."

"No indeed, sir," Apoojamy replied. "I would never dream of making light. I above all know . . ."

"Then you'll know that I will not be taking this lightly, Apoojamy."

"Almost certainly, sir."

"There is a Code, Apoojamy, outside of which is darkness and anarchy, without which enterprising men are unable to earn their keep, and put bread on the table, and store up against the day!"

"A most honorable Code, sir," affirmed Apoojamy. "Praise the king!"

"Praise him indeed," Joe Granbousse said absently. "And this Code, as I said, has today been violated!"

"Most viciously, sir."

"And I will be recompensed!"

"Yes, yes, yes!"

Bella suppressed a sigh. *When will these idiots shut up? I need a hit.*

"Now, Apoojamy," Joe Granbousse continued. "Let us be clear."

"Crystal, sir."

"You say that you spotted this fiend."

"Almost certainly, sir," Apoojamy declared.

"*Almost* certainly?" Joe Granbousse repeated.

"I am begging your pardon, sir . . ."

"Did you *almost* see him, or did you *certainly* see him?"

"Absolutely, sir. He was short and thin, like a stray cat, and his hair was tangled."

There was a silence. "Is that all?"

"He wore pantaloons and a linen shirt."

"By the Wind, Apoojamy!" Joe Granbousse roared. "You're describing half the boys and men in the Camp!"

Apoojamy whimpered.

"I know his shape, sir," Apoojamy whined. "I can exactly certainly spot the bugger. Of this I am certain."

"Fine," Joe cut in. "Let us go on a little further now, in case we scent smoke and locate the criminal. If so, we will execute justice.

If not, we shall bring the matter before the king in the morning."

"A most excellent declaration, sir!" cried Apoojamy.

Joe Granbousse's sigh was audible.

"I swear, Apoojamy," he said. "You have your head so far up my backside that sometimes I don't know my end from your beginning. Now, onward. I am tired and honest men need their rest."

The glow of the lamp faded as the two men walked on up the path. Rather than rising, however, Bella shifted herself into a more comfortable position and waited. Several minutes later, the light reappeared and floated back towards the flatland. The men were in full flow again.

". . . and so I said to him, I said, 'This is the finest stock west of the Tyrant's lands.' 'Then why,' he says, 'does it taste like paraffin?' He is not believing me, I can tell that now. So I say something about the cane and the soil in which it lies, and how sometimes this can add new flavors . . ."

"Indeed I remember it, sir," Apoojamy declared. "It was a most ingenious solution to your dilemma!"

"Then you will also remember that he didn't swallow that load!" Joe Granbousse snapped. "You will remember how he started threatening me! So I offered him a discount on the next flagon . . ."

"And he accepted! The same stuff too! Yes, yes. I perfectly remember. How utterly commendable . . ."

Their voices faded. Bella pushed her way out of the bushes and stood with her head tilted. Sifting through the din of the crickets to the moan of the onshore wind further on and the almost imperceptible hiss-and-suck of the waves over the sand, she could hear nothing that suggested the whining of petulant merchants and their squeaking assistants. She stretched herself, yawned, and ambled back down the path. Reaching the flats, she kept on going among the coconut trees until they fell behind and her feet sank into the powdery sand. Full in her face now, the wind was a single breath exhaled from the east. The open ocean heaved and hissed in and out over the sand, while the moon shattered into fragments over its surface.

Bella barely glanced at the sight—she was thinking about something else, and looking around for a place to light up. A large rock lay nearby, just above the line of seaweed. Bella made her way towards it as quickly as the clinging sand allowed. Relieved, she lowered herself down against the cool stone. She would stay dry when high tide came, unseen from the head of the beach.

At last, her hands shaking, she scrabbled in the pocket of her pantaloons and pulled out the item she had stolen from Joe Granbousse's storehouse—an oilskin pouch tied with laces. Opening it in her lap, she carefully reached into the sleeve and fingered the coarse grains of Dragon's claw, and then bent to inhale its biting odor on her fingertips. From her other pocket she pulled a small clay pipe with a silver lid clasped over the bowl. Quick with desperation, she filled the pot with the Dragon's claw, then pulled out a box of matches. She swore as the wind killed both the first and second attempts inside her cupped hands, before the contents of the bowl caught and hissed. Bella snapped the lid closed and sucked deeply at the pipe. The smoke raked at her lungs, and she shuddered. The pain took longer to fade than when she first used the Claw, but fade it finally did, giving way to the numbness she had been craving. Slowly, Bella exhaled as she sank back against the rock, feeling that her whole body was dissolving into its surface.

Perhaps I will sleep tonight, she thought. Not that she cared much either way. This would not be the first sleepless night of her life. For as long as she could remember, she had suffered from insomnia. Even among those faint outlines of her life before Mysterion, before she emerged from the Nightmare Tree, she could remember sitting awake in a dark place while two people shouted at one another somewhere nearby.

Couteau was a name she had given herself when she came to the Brethren, because she liked the sound of it. *A pirate should have a sharp name*, she thought dreamily, staring up at the stars that traced infinite spirals and trails across the black sky. Bella the Knife, that was sharp. She had proved it too, on countless occasions. *Bella Couteau—touch me and I'll cut you.*

When she came out of the Nightmare Tree, all that remained in place of her heart and mind was a dull cloud. She could think with a greater clarity than ever before, and yet nothing had any substance. Things and people, and even her own thoughts and feelings and actions, reached her faintly, from across the span of a vast abyss. So whether she slept or not any more, it hardly seemed to matter. Every moment had become little more than a kind of sleepwalking.

Bella drew deeply on the Claw pipe. The stars above had faded. The wind on her face was cool, tinged with the early morning. The tide had peaked. Spray touched her legs as the waves broke close by, but she made no attempt to pull in. The Claw was working its magic—her eyelids drooped. Then, just before she fell into oblivion, desolation swept in from the wings of her heart. The urge to cry out welled up in her throat, became unbearable, and receded.

Darkness came over Bella Couteau.

CHAPTER TWO

ÐISAGREE

Bella woke to a pinch on her hand. She dragged her eyelids open. A hermit crab had her thumb gripped in one claw. Irritated, Bella swung the crab against the rock behind her with a sharp *crack*. It released its grip and lay with legs kicking at the sky. Bella stood and dusted sand from her pantaloons. The sea was a red mirror. The sun had not yet broken the horizon. She looked over the water. Over there was the Tyrant's land. *The Tyrant and his slaves*, she thought.

But she could not summon her usual contempt, either for the Wind People or their tyrant Elder. Instead—she could hardly believe this—she found herself curious. What would it be like to live as one of *them*? She shoved the thought away. *What's the matter with you, Couteau?* She retrieved her Claw pipe from where it had fallen, and noticed the crab still wriggling on its back.

"Stupid creature," she muttered. Placing her heel in the middle of the crab's body, she ground it into the rock. There was something reassuring about the way it cracked and squirted under her foot.

She turned away from the sea where the sun was now rising, strode to the head of the beach and into the trees. She intersected the path from the night before and ran along it through the forest. The air, though humid, was still cool from the night. Once her stiffened muscles had eased, she moved quickly, her body refreshed from sleep and her head only slightly foggy from the Claw. The trees thinned and gave way to scrub. The path wound among granite boulders. Bella slowed only on the steepest parts, until she reached the pass that crossed to the western side of the island. Ahead, the path dropped away in sharp angles to where the forest began, and fingers of smoke and a pall of grey haze over the trees betrayed the presence of Hodoul's Camp. Beyond lay the circle of Hodoul's Bay, its green water enclosed on two sides by the sheer granite cliffs that curved together to a narrow mouth, where cannon emplacements bristled like the teeth of a barracuda, ready to welcome visitors from rival Brethren crews. From her height, Bella saw the sentries slumped back against the barrels, obviously asleep.

Within this natural fortified harbor floated the armada of the Brethren of His Highness, King Jack Hodoul. As the leader of the dominant crew, he commanded the largest number of ships. Dhows shaped like scimitars, squat square-riggers, corsairs and sleek schooners, their spars bare, rocked and turned slowly on their anchors. Their decks were deserted, and Bella frowned. *All the sentries sleeping!* she thought. *Leaving us exposed—slack dogs! I should report them for a whipping.* She wouldn't do it, of course. Some things might not be written in the Code, but they were just as sacrosanct. *Besides, he probably knows anyway.* No one had put anything over on Hodoul yet, at least not as far as she could remember. Some of the Brethren even believed he had bewitched houseflies to serve as his spies.

He's watching, she reassured herself. *One way or the other, he's watching.*

Leaping lightly from rock to rock, she followed the path down to the Camp. Just beyond the tree-line, the *boma* fence rose up. Thorns and vines, planted side by side years ago, had grown and intertwined into a solid wall that sealed off the Camp's western border. She wondered if this sentry was also asleep. She had slipped through easily enough last night, but daylight was a different matter. If they caught and searched her, she would lose the whole stash of Claw.

Angling off the path, she approached the arched wooden gate with the stealth of a wild creature. As usual, the carved doors stood open to allow early traffic with the surrounding camps. Unusually, though, only one sentry stood guard with a musket—an immense black man who resembled the overflow of an underground volcano. He wore nothing but a pair of maroon leggings and a bronze band on his upper right arm. His head was a gleaming cannonball. Seeing him, Bella knew why the king had assigned him to guard alone.

With a rare rush of affection, she abandoned all her precautions, pushed through the undergrowth, and burst out onto the path at a full run. The sentry, startled, brought up his musket. Then he saw Bella, and his round face cracked briefly into a wide grin before regaining its customary composure. He lowered the gun and stood waiting.

She stopped a few feet from him.

"Hello, Dis," she said.

Dis regarded her for a moment, then shook his head slightly, almost sadly.

"Dis is not my name," he rumbled.

Bella threw up her hands.

"Well, what kind of name is Disagree, anyway?" she cried.

"The one my maman give me," he replied.

"But it's not a name. It's something you do."

"It's a name."

"No. Smith is a name. Pillay is a name. Disagree is a verb, as in, I *disagree* with you on that point!"

"It's a name," Disagree insisted. "It's aristocrat."

"Here we go again," Bella said, rolling her eyes.

"It is," Disagree said. "One of my ancestors is a slave for a plantation man name of De Sagré. He change it to Desagry during British times, and me and all my *real* friends say it just as you hear it."

"You made that story up."

"I have no reason to do that."

"Yes you do—to be contrary."

Disagree chortled. "Well, I disagree."

"What about your first name?" Bella said, struggling to contain her laughter.

"I'm not using that one."

"Why not? It's a good name."

"Because it has bad memories in it," Disagree said. "Just like your real surname, Miss Isabella Mor—"

"All right, all right," Bella interrupted, raising her hands. "Leave that alone. Hello, then, Monsieur *Disagree!*"

"Hello, then, Miss *Couteau*," Disagree said with a smile.

They made their way to the gateway. The very first king had made it at the beginning of the Age, carving the frame posts with tangled snakes. Each of the gates depicted the semblances of two Djinn—massive horned figures encircled with the swirling lines of chaos. Over the centuries, the wooden surfaces had worn and hardened to the texture of grey stone. Bella and Disagree sat down against the arched posts.

"So?" Disagree asked, after a short silence.

"So what?" Bella poked at the black earth with her feet.

"You get what you want?"

Bella shrugged.

"They see you?" Disagree asked.

"Apoojamy came down as I was leaving."

"Oh."

"He didn't see me, though."

"How do you know?"

"I heard them talking," Bella said. "He thought I was a boy."

"Oh," Disagree said. "Well, good, then."

"Yes," Bella replied, meeting his eyes directly for the first time. "It was good."

Disagree did not flinch from her look.

"Probably not over yet, though," he warned.

"So?" Bella said. "I'll deal with that too, if I have to."

"You say it," Disagree said, looking away into the distance.

"Damned right," Bella said. "And there's no need to lecture me about it either!"

"All I say is I know the king, that's all."

"So what?"

"He knows you leave last night. Guaranteed."

Her stomach tightened in fear.

"I doubt it," she declared. "I'm too good for that."

"You think?" Disagree murmured, raising his eyebrows.

"And—" Bella hesitated. "So what if he knows? If he summons me, I'll come, that's all. I take an equal share, just like the others, and I'll stand on my own feet and answer for myself."

"You know," Disagree said, "He writes that Code . . ."

"I know that, Dis!" Bella flared.

"All right," Disagree said. "I just say . . ."

"I know what you're saying, and I understand!" Her voice was higher now.

"All right, then," Disagree muttered, lowering his eyes. After a moment, Bella looked away through the trees.

"Why do you always have to get so worked up?" she said at last.

"I just think of you, Bella."

"You think too much," Bella said, and then she glared at him. "Papa!"

"Huh!" Disagree sniffed. "If you are my daughter . . ."

"Yes, yes, I know." Bella laughed. "You'd make me a respectable pirate!"

"Better than wander around in darkness doing who knows what."

"I am not your daughter, Dis," Bella said quietly. "I'm your friend."

"Yes." Disagree nodded. "We are friends."

"So try not to worry like a papa, all right? I had that already."

"All right," he muttered. "Sorry."

"That's all right—my friend." Bella reached out and covered Disagree's hand with her own. They sat in silence for several minutes. Morning sunlight now fell in bright, dusty bars through the forest. Go-away birds shrieked and squabbled among the golden-apple trees. The cool of dawn was retreating before the hot bath of day. From the forest behind her, mongrels barked and a shrill voice berated someone. The sounds evoked a trace of last night's sadness. She began fiddling with the medallion around her neck. It was a single doubloon hung from a leather cord. Along with her switchblade, it was her only possession from before the Tree. She fingered the coin, wondering how many hands had caressed it before her.

"Dis?" she said at last.

"Yes, Bella."

Bella turned the coin between her fingers, loving the buttery smoothness of the ancient gold. "Have you ever got the feeling that you were someone else and you were watching yourself do things?"

"How do you mean?" Disagree frowned.

"Like you were inside someone else's head or something."

Disagree considered. "Not really. I always see with my own eyes."

Bella smiled. "That's for certain." She dropped the medallion back into her shirt and chewed her nail.

"What's wrong, Bella?" Disagree asked. "You're all right?"

Bella dropped her hand into her lap. "Fine," she said. "I'm hungry, that's all."

"I bring some breakfast with me," Disagree said, gesturing to a cloth-wrapped bundle tucked against the foot of the gatepost behind them. "I bring enough for you too."

Bella grinned. "Of course you did."

They ate fried plantains, dried mackerel, and fresh coconut milk straight from nuts that Bella climbed for in a nearby tree and Disagree opened with his knife. They had almost finished when they heard Herald Bouteille calling in the distance behind them. "Attend!

Attend! The king seeks challengers!" he intoned. "Attend! Attend! The king seeks a worthy challenger!"

Disagree and Bella stared at one another. Slowly, Bella wiped her mouth and breathed out. The last time the king had called for challengers, the winning challenger had earned the appointment of king's apprentice and had gone on to captain his own ship. *Apprentice to the king,* she thought, and shivered. This was the opportunity she had been hoping for.

Disagree broke into her thoughts as if he had overheard her.

"Perhaps it is not what you think," he warned. "Perhaps it turns out not as you hope." He was referring to the last-but-one winning challenger, Sartish, who had run away to the East shortly before Bella arrived, and whom the Cyclops had probably caught and digested long ago.

"I don't care," Bella replied, leaping to her feet and dusting herself off.

"What do you challenge?" Disagree said without getting up.

"For me to know," she said, starting up the path.

"You sure, Bella?"

Bella threw up her hands without looking back. "Enough! I'm sure, all right?"

"All right," Disagree muttered.

"You want to come and hear it?" Bella looked back at him.

Disagree shook his head. "I do enough over here. With the birds and the coconuts falling, I'm busy enough."

Bella laughed and raised her hand. "Bye then, Monsieur Disagree!"

"Goodbye, Miss Couteau," he replied softly. But Bella was already running up the path to the parlay square.

CHAPTER THREE

THE CHALLENGE

The morning heat soon slowed Bella to a fast walk as she hurried along the path. The first houses appeared among the trees—wooden shacks on stilts. Torn mosquito netting and shutters covered their windows. Thatched roofs sagged and rotted in patches, like the fur of a mangy animal. The space around each house was a chaos of overturned barrels, broken furniture, and garbage over which emaciated mongrels fought. Mosquitoes and flies formed a permanent cloud overhead.

Brethren emerged from the squalor as Bella passed, flowing together onto the path. There were men of every shape and color, but their unshaven faces, unwashed clothes, and stench had reduced them to a single homogenous mob. Their eyes contained the same dullness induced by addiction to Claw. Some of them nodded briefly at her and one another, but most fixed their eyes on the distance, jostling and pushing to get ahead, each man lost in a single-minded purpose.

The women too were identical in dirt-grey dresses. Although they walked together, discussing the king's call for a challenge, Bella knew from experience their camaraderie was an illusion. *Make no friends and keep your enemies within reach*—the older shrews had taught her this lesson soon after she arrived. So she walked by herself, not looking at or talking to them as she strode past. Her aloofness drew a shrill commentary:

"It takes a little more than pants to be one of the boys, dearie!"

"And you'll never have it. No matter how hard you try!"

A shriek of laughter rose up at the joke. Bella's face did not change, but her hand dropped into her pocket.

"Perhaps it's because she hasn't got much on offer," a young one giggled.

"Well," came a reply, "she may get a taker anyway. Some of them like the girlie boys, if you catch me."

More laughter. Without a word, Bella whipped her hand out of her pocket and turned on the latest speaker, flicking out her switchblade. The woman screamed and reached into the folds of her dress, but before she could find her own blade, Bella was on her. A whispering, tearing sound of cloth, and the victim stood naked, clutching the shreds of her clothing about her. Bella leapt at her next tormentor, slitting the dress off her back before she could run a few paces. She caught and stripped a third before she reached her house, and the last at her front door. Then she folded and pocketed the blade, and strode off along the path in silence, leaving her victims naked and cowering in a circle of jeering spectators.

A few minutes later, she arrived at the parlay square—a smooth patch of sand, twenty yards on each side. To the right, the breakers rolled in from the mouth of the bay and exploded on the sand. Lining the other three sides of the square and facing the coolest breezes off the sea were the houses of the most prominent Brethren families, whose bloodlines led back to the very beginning. Unlike the houses deeper in the forest, these buildings were clean, with wide verandas and roofs of wood tiles. Some even had sentries posted at their front steps.

At the far end of the square, shielded by a grove of lime trees, was the house of the king himself. Bella had never been there. Soon after she arrived, she had heard stories of Brethren who had approached too close, uninvited, only to disappear. One night, she had woken to the sound of screaming. Bella shuddered and focused her attention on the center of the square.

The parlay platform stood on pylons and above it, the skull and crossbones fluttered and flashed in the sun. Herald Bouteille waited there, tall, angular, and impatient, rocking from side to side as the Brethren flowed out of the forest and gathered into a jostling pool around the platform.

Running to the edge of the crowd, Bella eased her way in towards the platform. She did not jostle too hard, in case she provoked a fight. In spite of her care, she drew a few growls at her passing, but continued to work her way in until she reached a spot three yards from the platform where the crowd grew too dense. Push further and she would get a knife between the ribs.

Herald Bouteille strutted in tight circles on the platform now, hands still on hips. He resembled a rooster about to announce the dawn. As the trickle of Brethren from the forest finally slowed and stopped, the Herald turned to face his audience. He lifted his chin and silence descended.

"Brethren, I call ye to strength unbound!" he cried in a guttural bass. It was the customary formula for a challenge, and a cheer went up from the crowd. "Who shall prevail? Who shall be cunning? The one who pities not, or else feeds the worms! The king will know this steadfast man," Herald Bouteille continued. "He rewards him who will not bend! Who will triumph, who'll meet his end?" Herald Bouteille slapped his thigh to the end-rhyme. More loud cheering, which died swiftly into an expectant hush. Bella shivered. Now he would announce it.

"His Highness King Hodoul calls for a Brother to take a claw from Leviathan *without* breaking the Charter."

A second passed while these words sank into Bella's mind. A second, while she registered it, made the connection, and realized that the single greatest stroke of luck of her life had descended. She knew beyond all uncertainty that she alone could answer this challenge successfully. Her discreet inquiries had assured her that the secret she had been keeping now for several weeks, hoping for an opportunity to use what she knew, was hers and hers alone. *It's finally here*, she thought. Blood roared in her ears.

"It's madness!" cried Guillotine, a scarred, balding man who had grown and tied the remnants of his hair into a pigtail. His cry unleashed a storm of protest that broke against the platform in waves. The Herald was unperturbed by the threats on his life, the aspersions cast against his parentage, the calls to open rebellion against a king who no longer deserved the loyalty of his Brethren. He simply waited until they lost impetus, then raised his hand. The crowd fell into an uneasy, sullen silence, and Herald Bouteille regarded them calmly.

"The king is aware of the dangers," he said. More muttering, and he raised his voice. "But he believes that there is at least one from his crew who is worthy and able to take it!" Then, Bella saw the Herald's eyes come to rest on her. A prickle ran up her spine, igniting her face with fire.

He's waiting for you. He wants you to speak!

"No one's crazy enough to—" someone began. Then Bella raised her hand.

"Couteau," the Herald said. She was sure she could hear his relief in his voice.

She took a deep breath.

"I take the challenge," she said in a loud clear voice.

In the hush that followed, Bella could hear the roar of waves on the beach and the steady *thwup, thwup* of the flag above them. She looked straight ahead at Herald Bouteille, keeping him slightly out of focus so that she could not see his exact expression. But she could feel the eyes of the Brethren on her. They were not friendly eyes, and she thought: *Any moment now.*

"Bold little strumpet!" a woman shrieked. "Thinks she can come to an adult gathering and play us for fools—!"

"I have a right, like anyone else," Bella said, wondering if they could hear her voice quiver.

"This is a *challenge!*" a tall, sallow-faced man beside her replied. His spittle flecked her cheeks as he leaned towards her. "This is serious business concerning the king, not the fantasy of some fifteen-year-old twit who thinks she has inherited the powers of a Djinn!"

Bella turned and met his eyes, trying not to flinch.

"This is not a fantasy," she said. "I can do it. Can you?"

"I don't waste my time with madness!" the man cried.

"Get lost, Couteau!" someone called. "You're wasting our time!"

"Go dig a hole and bury yourself!"

"Jump off a cliff!"

"That's enough!" Herald Bouteille cut in. The noise subsided reluctantly.

"Come forth, sister Bella," said the Herald. With her heart stumbling, Bella walked forward, ignoring the glares and muttering as the Brethren parted for her. She reached the platform and hoisted herself up.

Bella now stood very straight beside the Herald, her chin raised. "You know how to say it?" the herald asked Bella in a low voice.

"Yes," she replied. And taking a deep breath to slow her beating heart, she cried, "On my honor, I take the king's challenge to get a claw from the Leviathan . . ." She paused. "Or die in the trying!"

"Our sister has challenged," the Herald said. "Will anyone else?"

A silence followed, punctuated by whispering. Then Guillotine grinned, exposing a row of gold teeth.

"Time to slap the upstart down," he growled. "I'll do it."

A ragged chorus of agreement.

"You also accept the challenge?" Herald Bouteille asked, throwing an odd, nervous glance towards the king's house.

"You can shove your proper order where no one would want to look," Guillotine replied. "Yes, I accept."

Herald Bouteille's voice rose above the cheers. "Very well! Call out the boats! To the North Point deep!"

CHAPTER FOUR

THE CLAWS OF LEVIATHAN

Of all the seagoing dragons in Mysterion, Leviathan had survived the longest. In past ages, at the turning of the monsoons, the Brethren had killed dragons for their claws in the western seas up to the edge of the Cyclops's territory, beyond which they dared not venture. In time, however, the dragons had withdrawn and become violent, their natural friendliness betrayed too often by the harpoons and cannons of the hunting parties. They had become so rare and difficult to find that only a few had the skill and patience to hunt them. These men had formed a crew known as the Claw-Men, devoted almost entirely to dragon hunting. They sold to whoever could pay, regardless of loyalty. In the king's crew, the Claw-Men had an exclusive contract with Joe Granbousse, which made him the most resented and sought-after man on the island—not to mention the wealthiest, after the king himself.

Of course, none of the king's crew would have paid Granbousse's grossly inflated prices for a few measly ounces of Claw had they only been able to hunt Leviathan. The ancient dragon's claws, estimated at five feet in length from point to root, would yield enough powder for everyone to smoke themselves into oblivion. And the bitter irony was that this abundance lay within fire-rifle-shot of the island. The first king of the Brethren, Bartholomew himself, had trapped and leashed Leviathan to the northern cliffs on a two-hundred-yard-long, six-inch-thick chain. At that point, the island dropped vertically into an underwater sinkhole, which formed a perfect run for the monster. Then Bartholomew wrote a Charter protecting the dragon from hunting, on pain of death. It was said he signed this Charter in his own blood.

Many believed that Bartholomew had acted in the grip of advancing senility, while others blamed it on his irrational affection for the creature to whom he had lost his left arm. Whatever the reason, Leviathan had been protected ever since. Those Brethren who were found within fire-rifle-shot of the dragon's run were hanged in the Parlay Square. Those kings who were foolhardy enough to try to revoke the Charter had been shot or stabbed in the dark, poisoned by their cooks, or simply overthrown in a bloody riot. Reasonable or not, guardianship of Leviathan had become the highest law among the Brethren and the sign of a true Brethren king.

※　※　※

THE FLOTILLA OF SHIPS inched up towards North Point, their sails flashing and their hulls heeled far over in the gale that roared around the headland, whipping foam off the green surface. Bella stood in the bow of the king's own sloop, *La Justice*. The jagged cliffs towered three hundred feet above her. Bella saw none of it. She had retreated into the mist of her memory.

Moments before they weighed anchor, the king and his guards had emerged from the royal house, marched down to a skiff on the beach and rowed swiftly to the sloop. As the king stepped on board, Bella knelt with the rest of the crew, waiting to see if he would approach her. But other than a nod at the general obeisance and a word acknowledging the Herald's murmured greeting, the king allowed himself to be escorted below without a glance in her direction.

Had he chosen her for the challenge? Perhaps he didn't want to make a scene in front of the others.

Enough, she scolded herself. *Concentrate.* But something else was bothering her. Following a respectful pace behind the king had been Joe Granbousse and Apoojamy. This in itself was not unusual, as the king frequently sought the merchant's counsel. Today, however, Apoojamy kept glancing in her direction. As the retinue crossed the deck, she met his eyes briefly. His eyes widened and she caught her breath. Then Joe glanced backward, frowned, and muttered something. Immediately, Apoojamy, realizing he had fallen more than two steps behind his master, scurried forward, and they disappeared down the steps to the stateroom. The crew returned to its tasks.

As the challenger, Bella had received the honor of commanding the king's ship, which exempted her from her usual duties. She paced the deck in circles, chewing on her fingernail and thinking furiously.

He recognized me! No, not possible. It was too dark. He couldn't possibly have seen your face, just relax.

To distract herself, she looked around for her opponent's ship. Twenty yards to starboard, a large dhow whose Arabic name meant *Tongue of the Devil* heeled away on the port tack. The squat shape of Guillotine pressed against the windward railing. He was staring out towards the two-hundred-yard perimeter where the green water spun in all directions, kicked into madness by the confluence of two currents. That was the pit, but no sign of Leviathan yet.

Poor Guillotine, she thought with a grin. *He's probably wondering what the hell he let himself in for.*

She felt sorry for him—not sorry enough, though, to tell him her secret. One night several months earlier, Bella had escaped the camp without being seen and crept up an overgrown path to the edge of the forbidden northern cliffs above Leviathan's run. She spent the nights that followed there, huddled under a scraggly lime tree, enjoying the wind that blew full in her face along with an uninterrupted view of the moonlit ocean and flickering lights from the islands where the other crews had their camps. She did not approach the edge of the cliff until a sleepless night when curiosity and boredom overcame her fear of heights.

Below, in the wild dark waters of his run, Leviathan circled and dove, his chain whipping back and forth. Turning onto his back, the dragon pedaled the air, like a dog scratching itself on the grass. Looking at those legs, Bella wondered at the immense curved claws that glinted in the moonlight. She wondered how big a bag she would need to carry the Claw they would produce. She would be richer than Joe Granbousse, perhaps as rich as the king . . .

At that moment, the dragon roared and leaped several feet in the air, all that his stubby wings would allow. He rushed at the cliff with a wake of phosphorescent water spreading behind him. Thinking he had seen her and forgetting he was chained, Bella leapt back. But Leviathan did not reach up to clamber up the cliff face. Instead, he swam directly into the cliff and disappeared. From her angle, she could not see where the entrance was. She assumed it was one of those cracks that split the rock face and ran deep into the island, wide at the bottom and narrowing rapidly as it went up until it vanished, making access impossible from above.

Leviathan did not emerge again that night. Two nights later, however, she returned to spy on him, and noticed that his claws had been cut down to the nub. Within two weeks, they reached the same length as before—almost five feet from root to tip. Then they shrank again, only to reappear seven days later. Only after the third time did Bella finally understand what was happening to his claws, and the realization gripped her with excitement. All she needed then was a way to reach Leviathan's cave, if only for five minutes. She'd be rich.

She had dreamed about it for days, imagining how she would do it, but always coming up short against the Charter and what would happen if she dared even to approach the dragon's run in a boat. And then came beautiful Herald Bouteille, with his cockerel strut and his "impossible" challenge, looking at her with the eyes of her destiny. Not to mention good old Guillotine, stepping into his doom right when he needed to. The best versions of her plan had called for a distraction, but nothing in her wildest imaginings came close to *this*. Bella shivered now in the gale, nibbling her nails. *And if anyone's smart enough to survive, Guillotine is.*

She followed Guillotine's gaze back towards the dragon's run. The Brethren's motley ships had roughly lined the perimeter of the two-hundred-yard mark. Bucking and tossing against the wind and the south-running current, they struggled to maintain position under shortened canvas. Bella examined their own position. The helm had followed her instructions, not allowing the other ships to get between them and the cliff. Still, they were not close enough— still fifty yards or more from where the glass-green waves slid up to shatter against the sheer rock.

She turned and ran aft along the railing to where the helm, a short slant-eyed man with hair and a goatee like black flames, stood with his feet braced apart against the weight of the wheel. He nodded inscrutably at Bella as she reached him, then turned his eyes back to the sea. Ah-Time was always the professional. Today, however, he would have to take a few risks.

"I need to be closer!" Bella said, steadying herself against the wheel housing. "No more than fifteen yards!"

Ah-Time shook his head.

"Too crazy," he said. "This is safe."

"I have the right!" Bella shouted. "It's my challenge!"

"It's my helm," Ah-Time replied, his face expressionless. "My responsibility."

Bella clenched her jaw.

"Then I relieve you!" she declared.

"You have your way," Ah-Time said, and dropped his hands from the spokes. Instantly, the wheel spun out of control, the deck tilting sharply as the ship bore away from the wind. Taken off guard, Bella dove forward. A wheel-handle slammed into her shoulder and she screamed, falling to her knees. A moment later, the pressure eased, and she looked up. Disagree held the wheel with one hand; with the other, he reached down and raised her to her feet.

"You didn't need to do that," Bella said, massaging her bruised shoulder.

"You supposed to get yourself killed," Disagree replied. "Not turn yourself into a wheel-jamb."

Herald Bouteille appeared at the top of the steps, and called:

"His Majesty asks that you not treat his ship so roughly. He says that he was gracious enough to lend it to you for this purpose, but he would like it back in one piece if at all possible!"

Some of the crew laughed at this, and Bella felt her face getting hot.

"Inform His Majesty that the deed will be done without harm to his ship!" she shouted at Bouteille. The Herald raised his eyebrows in disbelief, inclined his head, and disappeared below.

"And you dogs can just get back to work!" she said to the crew before turning on Disagree with a scowl.

"You're supposed to be in the rigging," she hissed. "Not playing papa again and embarrassing me!"

Disagree shrugged.

"No one else can get you out," he said. "Least of all you." And before Bella could open her mouth to answer back he added, "You go back to your craziness. I make sure you are close enough."

Bella glowered at him a moment, then turned on her heels and strode to the railing, where a coil of rope lay, and on top of it a large grappling hook. Bella knotted a hangman's noose around one of the cleats and then hefted the hook, swinging it a few times around her head before allowing it to drop to her side. When she was ready, she looked back at Disagree.

"Bear off," she called. "But don't *look* as if you're bearing off. I don't want Guillotine guessing anything."

Her opponent's ship was moving in the precise opposite direction to their own, bearing off on the port tack so that it lay broadside to the semicircle of wild water that was the dragon's run. Bella could see Guillotine gesticulating by the rail as several crewmembers hefted a skiff over the side. It hung there, ready to be lowered into the water, while Guillotine loaded a bundle almost as long as he was. *A net*, Bella thought, filled with admiration. *Good thinking.*

He might even stand a chance with a net.

"This is it," Disagree called to her. "No closer."

Bella looked. Thirteen yards from the railing, the open sea broke against the cliff at a line of rocks encrusted with barnacles and seaweed. One of these boulders looked to her as if it might hold the hook quite nicely. From there, she could scale the cliff to the cave entrance.

"Hold," she ordered.

Disagree spun the wheel and the sloop turned slightly into the wind, spilling her sails, slowing until she was locked "in irons."*

Guillotine was climbing into the skiff now. He was readying the oars, waving a signal. Lowered rapidly by the crew, the skiff dropped to the water in a white explosion. At once, Guillotine detached the ropes, manned the oars, and pulled away from the dhow into the dragon's run.

Bella lifted the hook and whirled it several times above her head before letting fly. The hook landed with a clatter against the outcropping, then slid off into the water. Cursing, Bella pulled it in. As the grappling iron rose to the railing, dripping, she heard shouting behind her.

"The beast!"

"Le monstre!"

Bella turned to see Leviathan break the surface in a mushroom cloud of foam and an acrid breath of sulphur and dead fish. His head was the size of a full-grown horse and seemed to have been welded from cast-iron scrap. Sharp wing-shaped edges adorned his smoking nostrils. Opening his mouth, he revealed rows of spiny teeth and roared. Fifty yards away, Guillotine stopped rowing and stared at the dragon. Then he was busy with the net at the bottom of the skiff. Herald Bouteille clattered to the top of the stairs and shouted at Bella:

"His Highness wishes to inform you that he does not wish his ship to be dashed to pieces on the cliffs!"

"Tell His Highness to get some guts!" Bella snapped, before she could stop herself.

The Herald looked shocked, but there was no time for apologies now. Bella turned back and tried to lasso the outcropping again. This time the hook held fast, sinking deep into the barnacles. Bella tied off the loose remaining rope, and then gestured Disagree forward.

"Ah-Time!" she shouted at the helmsman, who was leaning against the aft railing, regarding everything calmly. "Get on the helm, or you will be responsible for what happens when Dis lets go!"

Startled, the helmsman ran forward just in time to take over from Disagree, who came to Bella's side and untied the rope from the cleat. He seemed to know instinctively what she was doing, and Bella was grateful. Who knows what might have happened if he hadn't taken the helm.

Dis smiled. "Don't worry. I'm always here to hold your loose ends."

Bella rolled her eyes.

"Just keep it tight, all right?" she said.

Disagree grimaced. "Go. Just don't get yourself brained, that's all."

"Maybe I'm brained already," she replied, throwing him a grin.

Leviathan roared again, and Bella looked around. Guillotine was rowing backwards, trailing the net into which Leviathan had blundered as he tried to follow. The dragon rolled and twisted. His heart-tipped tail beat the water into froth as he tried to break free from the mesh, but he succeeded only in entangling himself further. Guillotine seemed to be waiting until the dragon was thoroughly incapacitated before circling back to try to cut one of his claws.

Clever boy, Bella thought. Then out loud: "But he'd better do it quickly." Leviathan would only be trapped momentarily before those claws went to work and he broke free, truly enraged. And once done with Guillotine as his main course, he would be looking around for some dessert. Her advantage, real as it was, would soon vanish, leaving less than even odds. Time was short.

Touching Dis's hand briefly in farewell, Bella grabbed the end of the rope and leapt over the railing. Swiftly, she pulled herself hand over hand towards the cliff, ignoring the pain of her bruised shoulder. Her feet kicked the tops of the waves, and occasionally the ship moved towards the cliff, immersing her to the waist, but Disagree compensated to raise her into the air again.

Within minutes she had reached the outcropping and was scrambling along the face of the cliff, barely aware of the barnacles that cut into her hands and knees and the soles of her feet, and the crabs that emerged from the crevices to nip at her toes. Every few seconds, a wave hit and rose over her head. She clung desperately to avoid being sucked back. Then she went on.

At last, as her shoulder, hands, and feet started screaming too loudly to ignore, the cliff suddenly opened. The waves ran in unabated, but from somewhere inside she heard a roar, and the cave mouth exhaled a breath of spray into the air. Fear clutched at her stomach, but she knew that hesitating now would mean facing something far more terrifying when Leviathan freed himself from the net. Taking a breath, she worked her way along the rocks and into the cave mouth.

❊　❊　❊

ON THE DECK OF *LA JUSTICE*, Jack Hodoul had emerged from below decks with his entourage. The king now stood at the rail and regarded the mouth of the cave with an impassive calm that belied his excitement. *Bold*, he thought. *Bolder than I could have hoped, my dear.*

"He's on him!" a crewman shouted from the bows. Hodoul

dragged his eyes away from the cliff. He realized that he had been gripping the rail in a manner that might raise speculations. Deliberately but not too quickly, he dropped his hands to his sides and strode across the deck. The scene there was not as intriguing as Bella's escapades, but it was certainly entertaining.

Leviathan had succeeded in binding himself thoroughly in Guillotine's net, and now the pirate had steered the skiff to within a few feet of where the dragon tossed in the waves. He stood, balancing himself in the bucking skiff, and Hodoul saw the tip and handle of the saw he had strapped to his back. Then, judging his moment, Guillotine leapt, landed squarely on the dragon's stomach, and grabbed a fistful of netting. Leviathan roared and bucked, emitting a cloud of steam—all that sea-going dragons could manage of their airborne ancestors' flames. Guillotine stuck like a horsefly. He maneuvered himself to where Leviathan's front legs lay bound against his chest. With one hand, he untied the saw and squatted. He grabbed one of the dragon's legs, and Hodoul drew in his breath as Guillotine began to cut.

Leviathan went mad. His claws tore through the netting, flicked Guillotine backwards through the air into the waves beyond the two-hundred-yard perimeter. The dragon then tore the rest of the net into shreds and smashed the skiff into kindling with his tail. Satisfied that nothing remained of the irritating opponent, he swam circles of victory, roaring and blowing steam. However, Hodoul had anticipated what would happen next. The king was already crossing to the port rail when Leviathan stopped circling, gathered himself, and made a run towards the cave, dragging a three-foot-high wake of foam and green water behind him.

Reaching the rail with his entourage straggling confusedly in tow, Hodoul leaned forward and hurled a thought towards the cave with all his strength: *Get out, Bella! Get out now!*

❋　❋　❋

DEEP WITHIN THE CAVE, kneeling among the fish-bones and shed scales, Bella heard Leviathan roaring and guessed that Guillotine's net had met its end. Time to leave. She grabbed the smallest of the objects for which she had been searching and tied it crosswise to her back with the loose ends of her shirt. She slipped off the ledge into the water and started back towards the cave mouth. As the waves rushed in through the tunnel, they threatened to dash her back against the walls, but she timed her movements in reverse to her entrance, anchoring herself to a handhold on the inflow before letting go and allowing the ebb to carry her outward.

She was almost out when she saw the head of Leviathan ploughing towards her, pushing a wave before itself. She screamed, kicking and struggling, trying to angle herself away from the dragon's path, but the tow was too strong. She was going to be swept directly into his jaws.

She felt herself slow. The ebb of the wave that was carrying her had met the counter-wave pushed forward by the dragon. Again she kicked and pulled with her arms, and this time was able to drag herself to the edge of the cave's mouth. Trembling, her stomach heaving with fear, she wedged herself into the crevice between two boulders. But she was barely able to take a breath before Leviathan roared again. He had heard her scream. Halting his forward rush to confront this new intruder, he now reared up, his red eyes glittering.

Following some instinct, Bella began to untie her prize from behind her back. But her fingers were clumsy with fear, and she only managed to get one end loose before Leviathan darted forward. Bella jumped backwards into the crevice just as the dragon's snout struck the stone in front of her. With a loud report, the rock split. As Leviathan pulled his head back to strike again, Bella untied the other end of her prize and gripped it at the base with both hands. It was a claw, about four feet long, silver and curved like a scimitar.

Leviathan's head snaked down from a higher angle. A moment

before he struck, Bella threw herself backwards. His snout hit, cracking the rock in front of her, and she stabbed the claw directly into his eye, the sharp edges of the base cutting into her palms. Leviathan screamed and reared back with green blood snaking from his eye. As he rose, one of his fins grazed Bella's foot, opening it in a gush of red. Bella shrieked, but her noise was drowned in the sounds of the dragon's pain. Seized by great convulsions, his body cleared the water, twisting in midair, somersaulting. Then he hit the surface in a thunderous burst of foam and steam, and with a slap of his tail, upended and dove into the unknown depths of the sinkhole.

Bella sat, staring at the place where Leviathan had dived, shaking violently, her breath coming in short gasps. The gale had died, leaving the water agitated but no longer tormented. On the edge of the two-hundred-yard perimeter, men lined the ships' railings, staring towards her.

She saw *Tongue of the Devil*, and wondered absently if Guillotine had survived. Then she turned her attention to *La Justice*, where the slight figure of the king stood amidships. *He came on deck to watch*, she thought with a flicker of pride. Behind the king was Disagree. He was shouting now, and gesturing. Then he and several other crewmen were lowering a skiff over the side. Disagree leapt in as soon as the hull touched the waves and drove towards her, ignoring the possibility that Leviathan might break the surface, more enraged than ever.

Same old Dis, Bella thought. *Always worrying.*

The weight of what had just happened descended on her. The edges of her vision darkened. She blinked and shook her head. The darkness spread. Dizziness overcame her, and she pitched forward.

The darkness parted in flickers . . . Disagree rowing above her, glancing down with dark eyes . . . the masts of *La Justice* framing a sky torn with red clouds . . . Disagree again, carrying her down steps . . . the king's voice ordering, "You will treat her in the stateroom, doctor, in my bed" . . . Disagree smiling as he laid her on something soft . . . a bitter, fragrant taste in her mouth . . .

Then the darkness fell decisively. She let go and sank away into unconsciousness.

CHAPTER FIVE
HODOUL PROPOSES

Bella opened her eyes. The great white eye of the moon stared down at her, framed by the porthole. From the way the cabin around her creaked, the regularity of the ship's movements and the gentle *slap* of waves against the hull, she could tell they were no longer in the grip of the North Point current. They were swinging like a gentle pendulum, back and forth around a fixed point. She thought, *We must be anchored in harbor. We've been back for a while.*

She sat up, examining the bandages on her hands and feet. The pain, faded now, throbbed with her heartbeat.

A voice rasped, "The salve contains a few special ingredients. Your wounds will heal in a matter of hours."

Bella peered into the far corner of the cabin, from where the voice had come. A match flared, and Hodoul's tousled head appeared, disembodied in the darkness. He touched the unlit cigarette dangling from his lips with the match. When the tip glowed evenly, he whipped the match out, and his face sank into an obscure dusk where only his eyes glittered.

"You slept a while," he said. "Making up for a few lost years?"

For once, she found herself unable to come back with anything. A nest of snakes had come to life in her stomach. Here was the moment and suddenly, all her planned-for sophistication vanished.

"You had a right to your sleep," the king continued. "It was a bold thing you did, Bella Couteau." He rose from the ornate arm-chair where he had been sitting and glided across the cabin to the porthole. In the moonlight, his face beneath the pile of curling silver hair was impossibly cracked and wrinkled, like a riverbed in a drought. His deadened eyes stared forward.

"Very bold," he said. "Perhaps too bold." He glanced at Bella and she felt a film of ice creep over her skin.

"You were aware of the stricture concerning Leviathan," he continued, his eyes snaking into her. "That he shall not be hunted for his claws, on pain of death . . ." He paused, leaving the last word hanging.

The ice on Bella's skin slowly sank into her stomach. Dis was right. This was not what she had expected.

The king took a drag from his cigarette, and smoke enveloped his face.

"You were aware of the stricture, were you not?"

Bella nodded.

"Don't you have a voice?"

"Yes," Bella mumbled.

"Then I repeat: Did you understand the law concerning Leviathan's claws?"

"Yes."

"But you obviously had a plan today, did you not?"

Bella said nothing.

"You had been planning to take his claws for a while, hadn't you?"

"No!" Bella said.

"Then what?" The king's eyes glittered through the smoke of his cigarette. "How is it that you had a plan?"

Her whole body was frozen now. "I was . . ." she started. "It was . . ."

"What, girl!" King Jack snapped. "Speak your mind!"

Bella took a deep breath. "I knew that he shed them every two weeks."

"And how did you know that?"

"I watched him . . ." She paused. "From the top of the cliffs above his run."

The king gazed at her expressionlessly, his eyes turned back to stone.

"Good," he said finally. "I was right about you. You are not tentative, and that is always encouraging."

As Bella struggled with this sudden change of mood, the king turned from the window and sat down at the edge of the bed. Leaning towards her, his eyes flared like gunpowder.

"Tell me something, Bella. Do you know why Leviathan cannot be hunted?"

Bella blinked. "Because King Bartholomew decreed . . ."

"Yes, yes. But *why*?"

"No one really knows." Bella hesitated. "But I think perhaps . . ."

"You think what?" King Jack leaned forward.

"Perhaps he wanted to remind us, I mean everyone who came after, that *he* was the one who did it."

The king leaned back and took a satisfied pull on his cigarette before pinching it out and flicking it into the corner.

"Yes, I was right about you," he repeated, nodding. "You are quite right. A little inexact perhaps, but quite right. My honorable predecessor—may his name be eternal—possessed a quality essential to any leader, especially a monarch of the Brethren: He loved power above all things. And what is power, Bella—may I call you that?"

Bella nodded and the king continued to answer his own question. "Power is not the ability to destroy your enemies. What good is that, after all? Once the opponent is gone, so too is one's power over him. But that Bartholomew was a cunning one. He understood that real enduring power lies not in destruction, but in *restraint*. A dead Leviathan is just another rotting dragon's corpse, white bones turning to dust, claws burned to smoke and inhaled and forgotten. But

Leviathan bound—" He paused and smiled. "Now that is a legacy of power that will always be remembered."

"Yes," Bella said, with a little more conviction than she intended. Listening to the king, she had felt the mist inside her part, revealing something bright and sharp, the thing she had been seeking.

"So you understand me, then," the king said, with a trace of amusement in his voice. Bella realized she had exposed her feelings, and her cheeks burned. She glanced away and shrugged.

"I think you do. You understand, otherwise you would not have done what you did today. Most of that bunch out there—" he gestured dismissively at the door— "would kill anyone or anything in their way to get what they need. But you understand the distinctions, the finer points. There is something—*considered* about your actions. That's why . . ."

He paused and fumbled in his pockets, finally pulling out a tobacco pouch. He began to roll another cigarette.

"That's why," he continued softly, "I chose that challenge for you."

Bella stared at him. Her thoughts lost all coherence.

"I have been watching you for some time now, Bella Couteau," the pirate king said. "Ever since I . . . ever since you came to my island, in fact. I watched your little nightly trips to the North Point cliffs, and I suspected that you had discovered Leviathan's secret." He laughed softly. "Did you think it was just some beautiful coincidence to be offered the very challenge you had been preparing for so assiduously? Please tell me you are not one of those romantic types!"

A thought flashed into Bella's mind and she spoke before she could stop herself. "So that's why the Herald looked at me like that," she said. "Because you knew I would accept the challenge!"

Hodoul inclined his head. "Very good. Yes, I told him you might well raise your hand. And you did."

"And what business is my life to you?" she asked. Bella felt cheated somehow, caught in a plan she had known nothing about.

She became aware that her medallion had slipped to her back and pulled it forward again. Instinctively, she felt around for the switchblade. There it was, still in the pocket of her pantaloons, along with the pouch of Granbousse's Claw. *Probably soaked and useless now*, she thought. The king watched her with faint amusement.

"Let's just say," he said, "that I have a vested interest in keeping my eye on potential problems. All right?"

Maybe Dis was right, Bella thought. *Maybe he knows about last night.* She shifted and pulled her knees up, wrapping her arms to hold them together, her muscles screaming. She gritted her teeth.

"Whatever you say."

The king cocked his head at her. "And perhaps you could be a problem still. Could that be, Miss Bella?"

What does he know? Bella wondered.

"If so," Hodoul continued, "you could fall a long way. Or—" He paused. "You could rise to the heights."

There it was again—the thing she wanted glinting like a diamond unearthed in her heart, just within her grasp. With an effort, she pushed aside her anger and hurt pride and looked directly at the king.

"All right," she said. "Tell me." *To hell with what he knows.*

"Good," the king smiled. "Now you will need to listen rather carefully. You have heard the name Jonah."

Bella nodded. Barely a year after she had arrived among the Brethren, she had stood on the beach with a crowd and watched as a towering blue flame in the west challenged the sun rising in the east. The news arrived almost at once: a great warrior named Jonah sent from the People of the Wind had destroyed the Nightmare Tree and cast the Djinn into exile. Later rumors told that this same Jonah had inherited the throne of Monvieil, the High Elder of Mysterion. Then a seeming contradiction: Jonah had fallen back into Lethes. The Elder had died and the People of the Wind were now leaderless, with only the Angeli guarding them.

"What you probably don't know," the king continued, "is that Jonah was no great warrior with some unknown magic at his command. He was a mere boy of fourteen, no older than you are now, and he came empty-handed." Hodoul paused, as if unable to quite believe it. "More than that, Bella, Jonah came looking for his father, who was imprisoned in the Tree. And do you know what he did? He offered to take his father's place!" The king nodded at Bella's shocked expression. "Cunning, eh? Brilliant, really. And that's what did it."

"Just that?" Bella said, incredulous.

"Yes. Because he did not sell himself to the Djinn, he was free, and the Tree could not contain him."

Bella was silent, trying to catch a thought in the storm of speculations that whirled around in her head.

"And now this same Jonah has returned. Yes, you are right to be surprised. Only a few weeks ago, it seems. And he has taken up the throne of the tyrant and is now referred to as 'the New Elder,' or some such nonsense. And that is where my particular need comes into play, Bella."

The king sucked on his cigarette and exhaled, all the time watching Bella through the billows of moonlit smoke. The cracks and wrinkles in his face seemed impossibly deep in the shadows.

Bella returned his gaze, thinking hard. *What could he want?*

"The simple fact is, I can't have this boy ruling the People of the Wind," the king said. "They say he is even more of a child than his age. A fool, slightly." He tapped his head with one finger. "And yet they maintain some sort of absurd loyalty to him, more even perhaps than the previous old fool commanded." His voice now took on a bitterly derisive edge that Bella had never heard before. "They seem to possess the insane belief that the more hopeless, hapless, and pathetic a person is, the more worthy of reverence he is."

Suddenly restless, Hodoul stood. He struck a match and lit a lamp on the bedside table. When the flame was burning evenly and an olive light touched the corners of the room, he met her eyes again. "You would think, would you not, that such folly would pose no problem for those of us who live under the assurance of law and order, but it is not so. In the past week alone, I have intercepted no less than five defectors who had somehow allowed themselves to imagine that *slavery*—" his voice rose— "is somehow preferable over freedom and power. Can you imagine?"

Bella shook her head, remembering how even that morning, she had speculated about life with the People of the Wind. It was a shameful memory, and she pushed it away, focusing on the king again.

"Exactly," he declared. "And to think that I had to subject those traitors to some unpleasant forms of persuasion, just so that their treachery might be concealed, at least until I have permanently solved the Jonah problem."

He was looking at Bella intently now. She thought: *Here it comes.*

"The solution came at last to me last night," the king said. "And you were the first person I thought about."

"What was it?" Bella asked. It felt as if her heart had come loose in her chest.

The king smiled. "I think you know already. Don't you?"

Bella hesitated. "You want me to pretend to leave the Brethren."

"Good," the king nodded. "Go on."

"And when I am there . . ." Bella's voice failed on her. She made an effort and managed, "You want me to—"

"Yes?"

Bella's heart beat faster. "You want me to take care of the problem."

Hodoul smiled.

"But how?" she said. "They won't believe me."

Hodoul's eyes crinkled, but he did not smile. "I leave that to your expertise."

"I'm not good at pretending."

"Oh, I think you are," the king replied. "More than you imagine. Besides," he said, glancing away at the door again, "you may find a motive yet. Sometimes help comes from unexpected places."

"I don't know," Bella said, a faint panic taking hold of her. "I don't . . ."

A quick series of raps came at the door.

"What?" the king bellowed.

Herald Bouteille's voice was muffled: "Granbousse craves a parlay, Majesty."

"Can't it wait?"

"No, Majesty, he insists on being heard now."

"All right." Hodoul sighed. He turned to Bella, suddenly brusque. "It's time to go, my dear. You will have to save your doubts for another time, I'm afraid. I believe we have pressing business now."

"But what about—"

"No time now. Put these on." He gestured at a white shirt and dark pantaloons draped over a nearby chair. "They belonged to a former protégé of mine who is sadly no longer with us."

Bella remembered: *Sartish. The deserter.*

Hodoul grinned. "Let's hope your fate only *seems* to follow his. I will be waiting on the main deck."

In the doorway, the king stopped. The light from the passageway framed his slight form and the explosion of curls around his head. Beyond him, Herald Bouteille waited anxiously, glancing behind him every few seconds as if expecting someone to ambush them at any moment.

"So you will join us in a moment, Sister Couteau?" The king seemed to be speaking for the Herald's benefit. "We wish all the Brethren to witness our commendation for your daring today."

"Yes, Your Highness," Bella said automatically.

The king nodded laconically and closed the door. Still trying to sort through a chaos of scattered thoughts, Bella slipped out of bed and pulled on her new clothes (slightly too big, but clean and neat) before trying to tame her hair with a silver-backed hairbrush lying on the dressing table.

In the stifling heat, she was shivering.

CHAPTER SIX
TURN AND COUNTER-TURN

Bella stood alone in a space on the main deck, surrounded by the crew of *La Justice*. Out on the water, the other ships, brightly lit with lanterns and torches, floated as close as they dared, their railings lined with men who strained to catch a word or a glimpse. Clouds had drifted over the moon and now the full weight of midnight pressed down on them, held at bay only by the torches set up around the deck. The wind whistled and moaned in the loose rigging.

Before Bella sat Hodoul on a low carved stool, with Disagree planted immobile behind him. The flat canvas pouch of Claw rested in the king's hands. His face was inscrutable as he examined it. To one side stood the pear-shaped figure of Joe Granbousse, while Apoojamy's head bobbed in and out from behind his master's bulk. Joe was grinning like a furious gargoyle.

Something cold gripped Bella's insides. When she had stepped onto the deck and saw the merchant and his assistant, she knew it was trouble. Two crewmen had found the pouch at once in her pocket.

"You are certain this is your merchandise?" the king asked finally.

"Whose else?" Joe snorted. "It be my oilskin and everything! And if His Majesty be trying to cast doubt—"

"All right," the king snapped. "We were just asking." He looked up at Bella for the first time. His eyes were stones.

"Foolish of the thief not to dispose of incriminating evidence," he murmured. "Foolish and really quite disappointing." Bella did not lower her gaze, but her insides twisted painfully.

"What do you have to say for yourself, Sister Couteau?" the king asked.

Bella looked at him wordlessly. She knew what she wanted to say—*the fat pig deserved to be robbed blind*—but she knew that it would make no difference now. She had failed her test.

She shook her head.

The king's mouth twisted mirthlessly. "Very well then. Let the law be read!"

Herald Bouteille elbowed his way out of the crowd behind the king, bearing a golden scroll before him like a standard. Strutting to the center of the deck, he pushed Bella aside. Solemnly, he unrolled the scroll, tilted his head, cleared his throat and began to read in a funeral voice, quite different from the chant he had used to issue the challenge that morning:

"Hear ye Hodoul's Law of the Brethren, as has been taught and handed down from the beginning in word and deed, and hereon inscribed in gold and for everlasting time by His Majesty, Hodoul, twenty-fifth King of the Brethren. These laws were and are and shall ever be binding on all who call themselves Brethren; that is, all who have thrown off the shackles of the Wind and its minion, the so-called Elder of the East—" a cheer went up from the men at these words— "and who now live for freedom by a strong hand and a cunning mind.

"In the first, be it known that all the Brethren shall obey their own captain. Disobedience is punishable by hanging. In the second, be it known that all the brethren shall tithe to the king and their own captain. The former shall receive a quarter of each share of prizes, the latter an eighth. Withholding prizes from the authorities is punishable by hanging or marooning. In the third, be it known that deserters will be marooned or hanged. In the fourth, be it known that thieves from among the brethren will be marooned or hanged . . ."

Fear clutched Bella harder. Joe's grin widened.

"That's enough," the king said. Herald Bouteille looked disappointed, but thought better than to object. He rolled up the scroll, bowed to the king, glanced archly at Bella, and retreated into the crowd. Silence fell, made heavier by the slap of waves on the hull. The torch flames rippled over the faces of the men around her, the lines of their faces traced harshly one moment, smoothed the next, eyes exposed and glittering, then hidden again in darkness.

"By the fourth, I want justice!" Joe Granbousse declared. "Let her be—"

"We will pass the sentence, thank you very much!" the king snapped.

"I be having the right—"

"No, you do not! You may have certain privileges amongst the men, but we are the king and we will dispense justice!"

Joe opened his mouth to reply, then closed it. He shifted with frustration, mopping his forehead with a filthy kerchief.

King Jack leaned back. "Sister Couteau, stand forward."

Wishing she could curl up and disappear, Bella squared her shoulders and met the king's eyes without flinching.

"We must repeat our disappointment," the king said softly. "Your actions today were worthy of all honor. We expected to commend you, to raise you above your low estate—" he emphasized the last words— "but instead, we must punish you for breaking the law. It would seem that meritorious actions should cancel crimes, but it is not so. The law is the law and must be upheld, for without this is darkness and anarchy." He paused. "Therefore, for thieving Monsieur Granbousse's merchandise, you will be marooned in the realm of the Cyclops."

Joe chortled, and a murmur broke out among the men. Bella could hear voices calling the verdict from ship to ship.

"Your Majesty." Disagree spoke for the first time, leaning forward. He had turned grey. "A word with you." The king raised his hand without turning, and raised his voice to continue: "However." Joe's grin faltered and silence fell.

"We believe that some recognition must be offered for this girl's bravery today. We have decreed marooning in accordance with the law. This is *not* a death sentence." He paused. "And if our sister should survive the depredations of the monster and somehow return to us, her debt shall be nullified." He raised his voice over the murmuring that had broken out. "She shall return to her former condition, blameless, holding all of the rights she has lost today, including—" he looked at Bella directly now, pinning her— "the honor she has rightly earned."

It's a reprieve, Bella thought wildly. *And if I can get through . . . !* Her mind spun. The fear that had paralyzed her now began thrashing around in her stomach, as if searching for a way out. Hearing the conversation rippling through the crowd around her and on the other ships, she knew the king had scored a coup. The men were going for it. After all, the decision made sense; it was just. Only Joe stared at the king with bewilderment spread across his face. He could not turn the tide of approval, but she knew he could be a real obstruction.

She waited. The king seemed to be waiting too. He was leaning back, watching Joe through lowered lids.

The merchant roused himself and looked around. He seemed to realize the mood of the crowd, and swung his head indecisively. Then he took a step forward and the noise faded away abruptly.

"It be not lawful for two people to be marooned together," he declared.

"Ah, give over, Granbousse!" someone shouted.

"Yeah, Joe, leave it alone!"

The king regarded Joe serenely. "We know the law," he said. "We wrote it."

Joe's eyes narrowed. "So she will be alone?"

"Of course."

"Your word before witnesses?"

"Our word."

"Pah!" Joe Granbousse spat in disgust. "Then your so-called generosity be meaningless! If she survives, I'll be kissing her hand myself and giving her a lifetime of my best Claw. Guaranteed!"

The king shrugged. "If you say so, Joe."

Joe spat again and pushed away through the crowd, shouting, "Lower a boat. I be having real work to do!" Apoojamy threw Bella a glance of prim triumph and scurried off in his master's wake.

"Clear the ships!" the king shouted. "Monsieur Disagree, you will stay at our side. Herald Bouteille!"

"Oui, Majesté?"

"Two rounds of rum from our personal stores for every man tonight."

A cheer went up. The Herald looked surprised. "You are staying, *Majesté?"*

"Yes. At daybreak, send a crew to sail east for the marooning."

Half an hour later, the last skiff pulled away towards the shore. *La Justice* was deserted, except for Bella and Disagree, who had not moved from their positions. King Hodoul, who now stood at the starboard rail with his hands behind his back, watched the departing boats.

"Monsieur Disagree," the king said. "Please take the condemned below and lock her in my cabin."

"Your Majesty," Disagree said. "I plead with you."

"I need to speak with you alone, Dis. Please do as I say."

The king's familiarity in speaking to Disagree surprised Bella. She glanced at her friend's face as they went below, but he looked straight ahead as they wove their way aft through the dimly lit passage until they reached the master's cabin door. As Disagree pushed it open, he spoke:

"Next time you listen to me. All right?"

"Dis, it's fine, really." Bella spoke urgently. "I can do this—"

"You think you can survive the Cyclops?" Disagree shouted. "No one done it before, in the whole history of the Brethren. From the beginning! And you think you, fifteen years old, you can do it?"

"Why not?" Bella lifted her chin. "I got Leviathan, didn't I?"

Disagree shook his head. "What kind of head do you have on you? Do you see this Cyclops monster?"

"Yes, I've seen him. So?"

"Fine." Disagree said. "If you don't live with your head straight, then you be someone else's food!"

"Fine!" Bella stormed into the cabin and slammed the door behind her. "Nothing like the confidence of a friend!" she screamed from inside.

❉   ❉   ❉

DISAGREE SIGHED and pressed his fingers into his eyes before going back up on deck.

Hodoul was leaning against the railing with a cigarette lit. He flicked the cigarette into the dark water. "Hello, my friend."

Disagree inclined his head. "Majesty," he said. "I cannot allow this."

The king nodded. "I know. Nor can I. You know that."

"Then—why do you—"

"Because she left the compound without permission," the king snapped, "and she foolishly stole Granbousse's product without doing what any sensible pirate would do: bury it somewhere until things cooled down!"

"You know she leave the Camp?"

"Of course I knew," the king replied. "Don't you think I am aware of who leaves and enters my camp at all times?"

"You cannot forgive her then?" Disagree said, after a moment of silence.

"I have to abide by my own law, Dis," Hodoul sighed. "I may be a king, but even I have no choice in that."

"Then what to do?"

"Nothing. *I* can do nothing."

"Then I desert," Disagree declared. "I do not let her die alone."

The king nodded. "Yes," he said carefully. "You must do as you see fit. For my part, of course, I will utterly deny hearing what you just said, which will be easy, since we have no witnesses."

Disagree stared at him.

"Is that why you do not let me speak back then?" he asked finally.

The king inclined his head.

"But if I come back with her, I am a traitor—"

The king smiled. "It will be one of my few acts of mercy. One, I think, that few would contest."

Disagree looked doubtful. "Granbousse maybe."

The king made a dismissive gesture. "Be discreet, that's all. Joe is far stupider than we can imagine."

Disagree was silent.

"Suppose the monster get the better of us?" he asked.

The king laughed and clapped his shoulder. "Go ashore, Dis. Make sure that we have a few sober men for tomorrow. I don't trust that Herald. I sometimes wonder if he's missing a few essentials."

As Disagree pulled away in a skiff, he looked up to where Hodoul leaned against the aft railing. A lamp hung from the yard-arm transformed the king's hair into silver flames. His face lay in pitch darkness.

"One way or another, you must take care of her, Dis," the king called softly. "With your life, if necessary."

"Always, Your Majesty," Dis replied. "Always I die a thousand times a day inside for that little one."

CHAPTER SEVEN
HIGH AND DRY

aves unrolled before the bow like ruffles on a blue silk sheet. Neither the trails of cloud streaming overhead nor the single foresail to maintain the ship's momentum succeeded in sheltering the main deck from the molten heat. Against the railing a few idle deckhands wilted, with dark sweat patches blooming on their filthy shifts and stained pantaloons. Despite their languor, however, their bodies held a listening stillness as they peered ahead—watching for something.

Bella, Disagree, and Hodoul waited at the bow. The king sat on his low stool, sheltered by the only available shade—a canvas umbrella propped behind him. Bella stood with the straightness of someone trying to fight back the weight of the sun with her body, clenching the rail with both hands and looking as if something inside her was freezing over. To her left, Disagree was a sweating mountain. Occasionally, he moved his eyes over her face, and when she did not acknowledge him, he glanced towards the king, who smiled thinly but said nothing.

"Sandbar!" The lookout's voice, thin and ragged, floated down from the mast.

Hodoul stood. "Where away?" he shouted.

"Three points off the port bow!"

The king squinted at the horizon, then looked at Disagree. Disagree nodded marginally. His face was granite.

"Make for the sandbar!" the king called back at the helm. "And throw up a topsail," he added to one of the hands. The man immediately scrambled up the mast. As a bright triangle bloomed above them, Hodoul strolled to where Bella stood. "It's time, my dear," he murmured.

Bella clenched her jaw and her hands, staring ahead.

"Don't make this unseemly," the king said. "It would not be worthy of you."

Bella turned to face him. "That bastard deserved to lose everything he got."

King Jack's lips twisted. "Well, that's the beauty of the law. It is blissfully ignorant of human feelings."

"What about everything else you said?" Bella demanded. "Meaningless?"

The king shrugged. "Perhaps I misjudged."

"You didn't!"

"Then prove it."

Bella broke his gaze at last and cast her eyes to the main deck, where the crew now watched intently.

"I will," she said. She strode amidships. The king threw a half-smile at Disagree as they followed her back.

"Launch the skiff!" Hodoul shouted. "Move, you dogs!"

Several hands scurried to man the ropes, hoisting the skiff into the air, swinging it over and down to the water. Bella leapt in, and the king tossed a gunny sack down to her. It contained a loaf of bread, a full skin bottle, a pistol loaded with a single shot—the traditional supplies for one of the Brethren who was to be marooned. In addition, the sack held a roll of coarse twine.

Hodoul now trained a pistol on her.

"If you would not mind . . ." he said.

"I've got it!" Bella snapped. She was already in the bottom of the boat, trying to tie the loose end of the twine to the drain plug ring. When the bandages on her hands came loose and entangled the knot, she swore and ripped them off. Seeing the dragon claw wounds healed as the king had promised, Bella unwrapped her feet, then finished tying the knot. She hurled twine directly at Disagree's face. He dodged it, the hurt almost hidden in the depths of his eyes.

"Monsieur Disagree," the king said. "If you would do the honors."

Disagree's eyes flared, and he opened his mouth to protest. The king looked at him, and the flame in Disagree's eyes went out. He bent and picked up the twine, enclosing it in one immense fist.

The king turned back to Bella. She had settled herself at the oars, looking up at them, pale and defiant.

The king raised his hand in a gentle salute. "Farewell, my dear," he said softly.

"I'll be back," she retorted.

"That remains to be seen," he replied.

Bella looked at Disagree, but he seemed to have shrunk into himself, leaving a mountainous husk behind. Her voice struggled to get past her lips and reach him, but she forced herself to hold it.

"It is time to go, Bella," the king said. "And don't try to untie the rope, or I will have to shoot you."

Bella kept her eyes fixed on Disagree, but he was far away from her now, and tears filled her eyes. *Damn you, Couteau!* she chided herself, blinked hard and pulled away from *La Justice*. As she rowed, the frail umbilical cord of the twine unrolled slowly from Disagree's fist, while he, the king, and the crew watched her, observing the silence due the condemned.

Any moment now, Bella thought. Looking over her shoulder, she could make out waves breaking on the sandbar.

The king nodded at Disagree, then turned away. Disagree, his face almost grey, crushed the ball in his fist. In the skiff, the twine came taut, jerking the drain plug from the hull with a loud *pop*. The plug and twine dropped over the side into the ocean. Warm water flooded in, and Bella strained hard at the oars.

The sea turned from blue to transparent. She could see the white sand bottom with strands of seaweed waving in the current. A hermit crab in a conch scurried for cover from a shoal of angelfish.

The water in the skiff now swirled around her calves. The hull grew heavy and sluggish in her hands. Above, the weight of the sun and the washed-out blue sky pressed down on her shoulders. Sweat poured in rivulets down her face and into her eyes as she dragged the craft forward.

The hull touched the bottom, then slid on, slowing rapidly. Bella rowed on, sitting in a pond of warm seawater with the gunny sack perched on her knees. A moment later, a crunching sound—the skiff had come aground. Clutching the sack, Bella waded to the bow and, balancing on the gunwale, leapt the last two yards onto a sandbar no larger than a standard doorway.

The sandbar would be her home until the currents washed it away. *Or until the Cyclops comes . . .* She pushed the thought out of her mind. Out in the deep water, *La Justice* was already rounding for home. They could not risk waiting this close to the Cyclops's realm. The mainsail was set, and fore and topsails bloomed with every second until she was heeling under the breeze, spreading a wake through the clear water. At the aft railing, the great black figure of Disagree stood looking back at Bella. She could still feel his eyes from this distance, and fought to keep from raising her hand. Then he shrank as the schooner carried him away. The hull dropped out of sight. The white triangles of the sails rested on the horizon, then sank away.

Bella stared at the place where *La Justice* had been. She reached into the gunny sack for the pistol. She examined it, ornate and glinting in the sunlight. She knew it held a single discharge for the moment when she wanted to be free from suffering. Or else, she thought, a single shot into the Cyclops's eye. She grimaced and shivered at the same time. One way or another, she would need that discharge.

Carefully, she wrapped the pistol in the loose hem of her shirt, knotting the ends to secure it. Setting her face against the emptiness of ocean and sky, with the distinct impression of being lost inside herself, Bella sat down to wait for death.

CHAPTER EIGHT
THE END

Bella scraped the mold off the end of the loaf and took a measured bite. She resisted the urge to stuff in the last mouthful. Chewing the bread more than she needed to, she held up the wineskin, now shrunken, and carefully shook it. She could no longer hear the contents. Probably two or three mouthfuls left, she estimated. No more than two days. It was almost over, either way.

"Good," she muttered. "This place is getting really boring."

* * *

THE FIRE OF THIRST WOKE HER. As she forced her swollen tongue across her mouth, her lips cracked—salty blood on her tongue. She sat up, squinting against the light that seemed brighter today. A few feet away, a hermit crab scurried across the sand, naked without its shell. Bella untied her shirt and freed the pistol. With the butt reversed, she snapped her arm forward, and the hermit lay crushed on the sand, its legs kicking towards the sky. Bella ate the crab on her hands and knees, feeding on the raw morsels of its flesh and sucking every drop of its fluids.

"I am sorry, my friend," she whispered. "It was you or me."

Later that day, she saw something bobbing near the edge of the shallows. She waded out into the warm turquoise water, and almost wept to find a coconut bobbing there. Using the skiff's prow, she succeeded in husking and breaking it open, salvaging a couple of mouthfuls of milk from the cracks before it drained onto the sand. The meat, scraped off with a shell, was achingly sweet and cool on her tongue. As deliberately as she ate, it was gone too quickly.

"One more day," she whispered. In response, the sea glittered mutely and exhaled on her a gust of damp salt.

✳ ✳ ✳

WIND ROARED OVERHEAD during the night. Bella opened her eyes and darkness pressed into her. The images of half-sleep—of Disagree smiling, Leviathan snaking down towards her—fled away.

Perhaps it will rain, she thought, adding ironically, *just in time*.

Then it happened. Something slammed down, as if a door had fallen on her, driving the breath from her lungs. As she struggled to turn over, suffocating in the stench of goat and decaying bodies, a hand closed around her—hard as petrified wood—and jerked her into the air.

The Cyclops had come for her at last.

Bella struggled with the last of her strength. The monster's grip tightened. A rumbling came over the wind: "Don't bother, Pretty." The blood throbbed in Bella's forehead. Consciousness faded.

CHAPTER NINE

A DIALOGUE WITH GRATO

Water rushed down over her head, cool and sweet. Bella struggled out of the hole in her mind, aware of a smooth rock beneath her and wind streaming over her skin. Somewhere nearby, palm fronds rattled.

The Cyclops's voice came again, like the sound of a collapsing cliff: "Wake up, Pretty." And again the water poured down. This time she turned and lifted her mouth to the solid stream, coughing and spluttering with each swallow until her stomach was tight and painfully full.

She opened her eyes and pushed herself upright. The single empty eye socket of the Cyclops stared at her through a row of solid wooden bars. Perched on a ledge, her cage was a cube of takamaka poles lashed with thick ropes. A giant coconut tree threw patterns of noon sunlight over the ledge. Below and surrounding her on all sides, the ocean spread and receded to blue infinity.

"Nowhere to go, Pretty," the Cyclops said, with a breath of abscessed teeth. "Those ropes are stronger than me."

A thought came suddenly to Bella, and she felt for her possessions. They were all gone—the pistol, the switchblade, even her medallion. Bella scrambled forward and slammed the bars with her fists.

"Where are my things?" she shouted.

The Cyclops chuckled. "After I am done, Pretty won't need them anymore. I will keep them safe for the little pirate!"

"But I'm not a pirate!" Bella said desperately. "Not any more."

"They marooned her, eh?" The Cyclops grinned. "Poor Pretty!"

"Stop calling me Pretty!" Bella snapped, touching the blond tangle of her hair. "You're blind anyway!"

"I felt that she's a girl and I hope she's pretty," the Cyclops replied. "Either way, she needs a bath!"

"You can talk," Bella retorted.

The Cyclops chortled. "It's my memories, Pretty. Memories of meals gone by!" There was a loud *snap*. A coconut dropped from the tree and bounced off the top of the cage. The Cyclops caught the nut in midair, cracked it like an egg against the ledge, and handed it through.

"A snack to fatten her up," he grinned.

Bella scooped the meat out, filling her mouth. She could already feel new strength seeping through her.

"Eating people is disgusting," she declared, when she had finished.

"So *she* says," the Cyclops replied. "I call it service to the Wind. Ridding the world of dirty things."

A squawk cut in: "Sophistry!"

Bella looked up. A giant parrot now sat at the peak of the cage, its charcoal feathers glinting in the sunlight. The bird's head was tilted to one side, regarding the Cyclops with a bright eye.

The Cyclops did not bother to raise his head. "Crato and his big words again," he said to Bella. "Always trying to make up for his size by using words longer than he is. Poor little Polly!"

"Oh yes, three syllables," the parrot exclaimed. "So big! Well, since it seems to challenge your intellect, let me offer you a little definition. Sophistry is the habit of using elegant words and phrases to conceal immoral behavior—such as the habit of eating human flesh. And as for being *poor*," it continued, "I must be poor indeed to be friends with a thing like you!"

The Cyclops waved dismissively. "Ah! Admit it—what would you rather be doing than scolding me?"

"Probably enjoying a nice overripe mango on Monvieil's Island."

"Now who's lying?" the Cyclops chortled. "Nothing's sweeter for a little bird than to feel bigger than a Cyclops!"

Bella interrupted: "Perhaps you two should go and argue somewhere else."

The Cyclops faced her. "Now look what you've done, Crato! You've made Pretty want to get eaten sooner."

Bella made her voice as calm as she could. "If you're going to eat me, then do it and stop playing games."

"Well said, well said!" Crato squawked.

"Not yet, Pretty." The Cyclops shook his tangled curls. "Too scrawny yet for a good meal. A few more days of coconuts and roasted fish, and I can enjoy her best. Until then, she must be patient. Now," he said, "what does she say to a nice red snapper sprinkled with sea salt, hmm?"

"You can shove your red snapper," Bella replied.

The parrot clicked its beak in disapproval and the Cyclops wagged his finger. "Tsk, tsk. Pretty needs a bath on the inside too, I think. Too bad. Well, we'll see if she changes her mind when she gets a whiff of roasting fish in her nostrils! I'll be back," he said to Crato. "You keep a watch on her, old friend. Not to show pity, now!" His head disappeared below the ledge. A few minutes later, Bella saw him wading waist deep in the blue ocean. He stopped, his head swinging, listening. Then he moved on to the left, stopped, listened some more. Then he waded out, further and further, until he was a mere speck on the glittering expanse.

Bella looked up at Crato. The parrot was watching her with his head cocked thoughtfully to one side.

"Can you help me?" she said.

The parrot cracked its beak and ruffled its feathers. "I wish I could, my dear. I really wish I could. But there are moral considerations. On one hand, my friend's behavior, indefensible indeed; on the other hand, the greater evil of releasing you. Who knows what havoc you might wreak, what seeds of confusion you might sow, and the People are weak enough as it is."

"But I'm escaping," Bella interrupted. "I can't be all bad."

Crato cocked his head to the other side.

"They marooned me because I wouldn't follow their stupid Code," Bella continued, gratified to hear the real bitterness in her tone. "I'm sick of that life. Nothing but fighting and drinking and getting drugged all the time." *I'm good,* she thought. *I'm almost believing it myself.*

"Disgruntled pirate, eh?" Crato whistled. "I saw it once before. *Once.* And he turned out, though not without his own struggles, all of which seem to prove the rule that you can rarely trust a pirate. And even if you are sincere, experience has taught me that disgruntled persons are always so, no matter in what company they may find themselves. After all, my dear, do you imagine there are no rules among the People? If you think so, you will be sorely disillusioned. There are rules, some of them more difficult than those you are accustomed to."

"I don't care," Bella said. "I just want a new life." *Was that too much?*

Crato shifted from one foot to the other and craned his head out to sea. The Cyclops had moved in closer to shore. He spread his arms and a net sailed into the air, breaking the water as it hit.

Sensing the parrot wavering and realizing she did not have much time, Bella filled her voice with as much pleading as she could: "Please, Monsieur. Don't let me die before I can change my life."

"I don't know . . ." Crato's head turned left and right, as if seeking a way out. "I would need a guarantee."

"I swear—"

"Not enough!" the parrot snapped. "I would absolutely require a third party—"

A familiar voice interrupted: "I guarantee her."

"Dis!" Bella spun around and dove against the bars. He was squatting beside the coconut tree, his black face typically impassive. As he reached out his hands to grip hers, she wrinkled her nose.

"You smell like a toilet. Worse!"

Dis grinned. "I swim here so he can't smell me come. Then I wait and watch. I see where he goes to the head, you know, near his cave. It's the only way I can get in here without him knowing."

Bella looked aghast. "You mean that you put his…on your skin?!"

"Who are you, sir?" Crato demanded, his feathers ruffling to double his size. "Declare yourself immediately!"

"Calm down. He's my friend," Bella said.

"Calm down!" screeched the parrot. "Another pirate intrudes and you ask me to calm down. And he's the one you would offer as a guarantee? Laughable! One liar offering his word for another."

"Don't you dare call my friend a liar!" Bella shouted.

"Hah!" the parrot scoffed. "And why not? Did you ever hear of an honest pirate?"

"Bella!" Disagree hissed. "The Cyclops!"

Below, Bella saw the Cyclops, now standing motionless in the water, his head turned to face them.

"Damn," Bella whispered. She turned to Disagree. "Do something."

Disagree raised one hand to the parrot. "Now listen, my friend. Just listen."

"Listen?" Crato hopped from one foot to the other. "Listen to what? And don't call me your friend!"

Below, the Cyclops had begun wading back towards the island, kicking up waves with every stride.

"A trade," Disagree said. "I want a trade. Me for her."

"What?" Bella cried.

Crato stared down with his beak half-open. He looked as if he had been killed and stuffed on the spot.

"You want to take her place?" The parrot's words emerged as a whistle.

Disagree nodded. "I stay. She go home. My word on that."

"Dis, no!" Bella said. "I won't do it!"

"You go back," Disagree said calmly. "The king forgive you."

"But I have things to do first!"

"What things?" Crato interrupted sharply. "Mischief? Is that it?"

Bella glanced up at the parrot and then back at Disagree.

"I just don't want to go back," she said quietly.

"Your choice," Dis replied. "You stay here, if you want."

Bella gaped at him. "You'd rather see me *eaten* than go on?"

Disagree shrugged. "As I say—your choice."

"Crato!" the Cyclops bellowed from below. "What's up there?"

"Decide now," Disagree said to Bella.

Bella glared at him and gritted her teeth.

"Fine," she said.

"Okay?" Disagree looked up at Crato.

The parrot hesitated, then twitched and stretched his head over the ledge.

"Nothing!" he squawked shakily. "Nothing's up here!"

"Something wrong," the Cyclops said. "Something wrong in your voice!"

The sound of rocks tumbling against each other rose up at them.

"He's coming, by the Wind!" Crato moaned. "Oh, I knew this was unsound. I knew it from the beginning!"

Disagree was already squatting, getting his weight under the wooden bars. As he took up the strain, his face grew blacker and sinews stood out on his neck. The bottomless cage rose a few inches off the ledge. Crato squawked and flapped into the air, rising to perch at the top of the coconut tree.

"Now," he grunted. "Slide out."

Bella found herself shaking. "I can't," she said. "I can't let you do this."

Disagree swore and pushed the cage up several more inches, then slipped under before releasing his hold. As the cage crashed down, Disagree immediately enfolded Bella in his arms. Overwhelmed by the stench that covered his body, Bella held her breath, trying to control her gagging reflex. Then the Cyclops's head rose above the ledge, his single eyebrow condensed.

He sniffed and recoiled slightly. "Crato!"

"Yes?" Crato's voice, sounding timid, floated down from the top of the tree.

"Get your tail down here!"

The parrot, looking distinctly ruffled and nervous, perched at the peak of the cage.

"Where's Pretty?" the Cyclops demanded.

Crato looked down to where Disagree crouched over Bella, shielding her from the Cyclops's nose at the back of the cage.

"What do you mean?" the parrot sounded confused. "She is still there. And—"

"And what?"

"Her . . . friend," stuttered the parrot. "He came to rescue her, but then he went in with her instead and . . ."

The Cyclops leaned forward and sniffed, then looked up at Crato. "Are you playing games with me, Crato?"

"No, they're in there. Both of them! Say something!" Crato shouted down at Bella and Disagree.

Disagree smiled at Bella and touched his finger to his lips. Bella nodded and stuck her tongue out at Crato.

"You let them out," the Cyclops said. "Didn't you?"

"No!" the parrot shrieked.

"Tell me the truth!"

"I swear they're in there! Say something, you degenerates!"

"Then why can't I smell her?"

"Because her friend rolled in your filth, and you can't smell either of them under your own disgusting stink!"

The Cyclops considered this for a moment. Disagree gave Bella a look that said: *Get ready, any moment now.*

"There's only one way to find out," the Cyclops declared, and lifted the cage aside as Crato fluttered upward.

"Now," Disagree muttered, and they both scrambled backwards as the Cyclops's free hand swept over the ledge.

"So then, where is she?" the Cyclops roared.

"They're out! They're out!" Crato shrieked. "Oh, you idiot!"

Bella and Disagree slipped round the back of the tree, where fallen coconuts lay scattered at the base of the trunk. Disagree handed her a smaller-sized nut, just big enough to get her fingers around.

"Go for the eye socket," he murmured. "It's soft."

The Cyclops, still feeling around on the ledge for Bella, lifted his head sharply.

"Who's that?" he shouted.

"I told you, you fool," shrieked Crato, darting in crazy circles. "It's her friend, it's her treacherous friend!"

The Cyclops tossed the cage away down the slope and groped around the tree, trying to get at Bella and Disagree. But his body was positioned awkwardly, and they easily dodged his clutches. He roared in frustration, grabbing the tree to pull himself closer. As he did so, Disagree drew a tiny dagger from his pantaloons and buried it in the monster's finger. The Cyclops screamed and slid back down the slope, losing the ground he had gained. He ripped the dagger out, sucked his finger and pinched off the blood before scrambling upwards again.

"Hit him before he gets up!" Disagree shouted. With a coconut in each hand, he ran out onto the ledge, Bella following closely behind. At that moment, Crato swooped down at them, flapping in their faces, pecking at Disagree's head while hurling abuse in words that multiplied syllables and obscured meanings by the moment. Bella darted around the parrot, her throwing arm cocked. Reaching the edge, she saw the pile of tumbled rocks that was the island below her; the waves exploding green and white; and several abandoned boats with oars or tattered sails strewn above the break line. Then the Cyclops's face rose into her vision.

"There you are, Pretty!" he cried. "Nice to smell you again!"

Ignoring the stench that threatened to stupefy her and dull her movements, Bella whipped the coconut directly into the monster's eye-socket. It struck dead center with a dull, slightly wet sound.

The Cyclops stopped abruptly. He reached up with both hands and caressed the socket. He swayed on his feet.

Smoothly, Bella hurled her second coconut, and for a moment, the Cyclops had a grotesque coconut-eye. Then the nut fell away and the Cyclops collapsed backwards with blood streaming from the corners of his socket. His legs gave way and he tumbled at an angle down the slope, his arms splaying woodenly in all directions. Rolling through and crushing several boats at the water's edge, he finally came to rest with his body half in and half out of the breakers.

Behind her, Crato let up his attack on Disagree. He swooped over Bella's head and down to perch on the monster's chest, pecking at him, trying to rouse him, for once incoherent with grief. Disagree, dabbing at his bleeding head, came up beside Bella, and they watched the parrot mourn.

"Is he dead?" Bella asked. The rush of energy in her blood was ebbing.

Disagree nodded. The parrot's cries had faded. He now wandered in circles over the Cyclops, his body hunched.

"Everyone have someone who love them," Disagree said. "Even that one."

The words disturbed Bella, but she dismissed them with a shrug.

"You watch yourself again." She could feel Disagree's eyes.

"What?"

"I think you know. You watch yourself from the outside and pretend."

"I don't care what you think I am," Bella replied. "I fixed the monster, once and for all. The king will be happy. So whatever you think I'm pretending, it's all good enough for me!"

Disagree was regarding the parrot and the Cyclops again.

"So you go back then?" he asked. "To the king?"

Bella folded her arms and turned her eyes to the horizon. "I can't."

"I know you do this," Disagree declared. "I know you go back on your word."

"I didn't go back on anything!" Bella shouted. "I stayed in the cage, didn't I?"

"So what's so important to go on?" Disagree said angrily.

She clenched her jaw and fixed her attention on the horizon. He waited.

"Just something I need to do," she muttered finally.

"For him?"

"Yes."

"Huh! Prove yourself again. Good for you!"

"Shut up!" Bella said. "I have to do it."

"No. He say if you survive the monster, you can come back."

Bella shook her head, her eyes full of tears now. "That's not enough. He wanted more for me than that."

Disagree sighed and shook his head. "Always more, it seems. Well, I don't stop you. I do what I need to."

Bella glanced sideways. "You didn't need to come."

"Yes I do. He *tell* me to."

"The king told you?" Bella forgot her anger at this information. *He wanted me to escape the Cyclops! He wants me to go on to Monvieil's Island!* A flame of confidence flared to life inside her.

She wiped her eyes of the tears that had threatened to rob her of control.

"He wants you back," Disagree said. "What else do you want now?"

She regarded him calmly. "Just this one more thing, Dis."

"And you don't tell me what is it?"

"I can't say until it's done." Bella looked at him. "Try to understand."

Disagree was silent with disapproval.

"Go then," he said. "But I go home now. Perhaps I see you one day. Over or under the earth, I don't say."

❋ ❋ ❋

DISAGREE RINSED HIMSELF off at the water's edge. They picked their way along the shore, examining the abandoned boats. Disagree chose a light skiff whose sail was almost intact, Bella a single-outrigger canoe with a ragged lateen. They began loading their respective boats with coconuts, taking trips back and forth to the tree, which turned out to be the only one on the island. Neither of them spoke, though Bella occasionally threw covert glances at Disagree, wondering when he was going to try for the last word. But Disagree had sunk into himself, and he maintained the silence of an extinct volcano.

When the tree was stripped of nuts and they each had a fair supply, Disagree inclined his head at her and led the way up the slope. The Cyclops's lair was a long, low hollow among the rocks. From the ceiling hung coir ropes of salted dried fish, while the entire floor was taken up by a stained coir mattress. As they approached, the smell hit Bella like the Cyclops's hand, and her gorge rose. Disagree did not pause, ducking inside. Bella took a deep breath before following, her stomach heaving every time she was forced to inhale.

They found the Cyclops's cache buried inside the mattress—

knives and swords, guns, clothing, and jewelry. To her delight, Bella found both her switchblade and her medallion at the top of the pile. In addition, she armed herself with a brace of pistols, a bag of fireballs, and a coil of sturdy rope.

After finding and discarding several items, Disagree changed his soiled pantaloons for another, slightly tighter pair with red stripes. He chose a machete whose blade he tested on his thumb, as well as a wide-brimmed straw hat. Noting the wisdom of that last choice, Bella also found a hat—an old-fashioned tri-corner that fitted her nicely. Then she followed Disagree in filling her arms with dried fish. Grateful to escape the stench of the cave, they returned to the beach.

The tide was falling, and the Cyclops was now firmly lodged among the rocks. Crato was nowhere to be seen. *So much for caring,* she thought. *He probably stuck around just for the handouts.*

Disagree spoke directly to her thoughts. "He probably goes to warn them. They know you come now."

"I'll take my chances," she replied.

They launched their boats in silence. As she clambered in, Bella felt immediately satisfied at how her dugout handled under sail. Though torn through in several places, the canvas caught and held the wind, swiftly driving the knife-like hull through the clear green water. In the past weeks the wind had finally set out of the southwest, and it would stay there for months to come. With luck and barring a squall, she could run the dugout all the way to Monvieil's Island.

She looked back. Disagree had set his sail to a close reach, the skiff slipping away at almost a right angle to her while he regarded her over his shoulder, sad in the way that only a stone can seem sad.

Perhaps he won't say anything, she thought, and suddenly, she felt bereft.

Disagree called, "Not just you have secrets. With this or without this, you are a great treasure to him."

Bella frowned. "What do you mean?"

"I keep my secrets too," Disagree replied. "You can find out in time."

He turned to watch the horizon ahead. The gap between them widened rapidly. Bella had the urge to turn the dugout, but she resisted. *It's his last ruse*, she thought. *Try a bribe when all else fails.*

"I suppose I will," she called. "Goodbye, Dis."

Disagree kept on sailing. His silence hurt her, but not enough; she turned her attention to her boat, now watching the pontoon cutting white lines in the water, now turning her eyes to the triangle of the lateen sail, as the monsoon drove her on towards the east in a single, endless breath.

CHAPTER TEN

THE RETURN OF DISAGREE

L ike the shadow of a mountain, Disagree emerged from the trees. The king's house was lit up on all sides by oil lamps hanging from the eaves. Clouds of insects circled the lamps, some throwing themselves at the glass, sizzling as they hit. The sentries' hands went for their rifles, then relaxed when they saw Disagree. One gestured at the back door with his head:

"He's taking care of someone in the basement. He said come down if you want, or wait in the kitchen."

Disagree grimaced. He had seen too much of what the king did in the basement to have any interest in it. Hodoul must have known how he felt, to give him the option of staying in the kitchen.

Only the dim echo of the veranda lamps relieved the darkness of the back corridor. Disagree paused to glance into the room where the king slept and noticed the coir mattress dragged to one side. A faint square line of light betrayed the trapdoor set into the floor. From below a faint rhythmic *thwup* rose up. That and nothing else. He grimaced again: *Nearly done with him.*

Disagree slipped into the kitchen and sat at the far corner of the table. He thought alternately about Bella—how she was making out—and the poor wretch hanging in the basement. The last two times the king had administered Mose's law, the prisoners had almost died. That silence did not bode well.

A few minutes later, he heard footsteps rising from below in the next room. The back door swung open.

"Get him out," came the rasp of Hodoul's voice. "And make sure he lives to tell what happens to deserters."

Hodoul strode into the kitchen a moment later, carrying a long heavy cane with bumps along its length. He glanced in Disagree's direction, but did not acknowledge him. Dis knew better than to think that Hodoul had not seen him. *Perhaps he is angry I did not come down.* Going to the sink, Hodoul ran the water over the cane, running one hand slowly up and down the shaft. Then he turned off the faucet and left the cane to dry on the edge of the sink. He came over and lit a lamp hanging over the kitchen table. The light flared and flickered, and the first thing Disagree noticed was the spots of blood that dotted the king's white shirt.

"Don't start with me," the king said. "I don't have the luxury of your mercy." Hearing something in Hodoul's voice, Disagree raised his eyes to that angular, ruined faced with its mountain of silver curls. In the grey eyes, dead to anyone else, he recognized a faint but definite anxiety.

He is not angry, just worried about Bella.

"Where is she?" the king said.

"She does not come back. She says she have something to do for you."

The expression on the king's face did not change, but there was a faint easing of tension in his body.

"And the Cyclops?"

"Dead."

The king was silent. "So where did she go?"

Disagree looked at him. "She go on. She say, something she must do for you."

Hodoul smiled. "I suppose you want to know what it is."

Disagree said nothing.

"I need to test her," the king said. "I need to see. Those men will

eat her alive if she is not ready. You know the things I have to do."
He looked towards the corridor. "Would she do them?"

"Perhaps she does not need to do them."

The king's eyes narrowed. "What are you saying?"

"Perhaps you can leave her alone—"

"Never," Hodoul hissed. "I will not go down to dust! Not after all this!"

Disagree knew better than to pursue this particular point.

"And you will respect my plans," Hodoul continued, his eyes baleful.

"Of course, Majesty," Disagree murmured. "Always—you know."

The king's eyes softened.

"Yes," he said. "I know. But you seem to forget yourself sometimes."

"That little one. She makes me forget."

"I can't afford that." Hodoul chuckled. "I suppose that is why I am king. Now," he went on briskly, "we have work to do. I want you to go and parlay with the other crews. Apprise them of the Cyclops situation and propose a combined raid. We all meet at the monster's island and sail on to the East, portions to be assigned according to our agreed treaties. All right?"

"What about the Angeli? Perhaps they try to stop us?"

The king grinned and shook his head. "They do not fight human flesh, remember? They may assist the People of the Wind, but if my memory of history is correct, it will make no difference in the end."

"So you want me to go now?"

"Yes, now. Are you tired?"

"I sleep a little already."

Hodoul put his hand on Disagree's shoulder. "Rest a little in my room if you want, then go. We sail with the tide."

CHAPTER ELEVEN

TALA-QATALA

Day after day, the waves followed her in procession, each one sweeping forward to tilt the dugout down its face, the bow throwing up wedges of foam before the crest slid amidships and the boat came level. Then the wave surged ahead, and the dugout tossed back, the sail collapsing, then snapping full as the next wave came forward and the wind drove her onward again.

Bella sweltered through the mornings under the shade of the lateen, with her tri-cornered hat pulled over her face. The worst came at noon, when all shade vanished and the sun beat directly overhead. Some days clouds sailed up from the horizon and piled into thunderheads before unleashing a rainstorm. Then Bella put out empty coconut shells to collect water, and having satisfied herself that only the fish could see her, she bathed, spreading her clothes under the downpour.

The rain let up abruptly, as if someone had stopped working a pump. Bella beat some of the water out of her clothes and dressed, sighing at the coolness on her skin. A shell brimming with rainwater was a welcome relief from coconut milk, and still sipping, she settled with her feet in the warm ocean to watch the sun exploding into colors on the horizon behind her.

At those times, Bella thought about Dis. They had often watched the sunset, eating the sweet meat of the jackfruit and competing to see who could spit the seeds the furthest. She missed his presence now, and kept glancing around, overcome by an inexplicable sense of imbalance.

Dis had been the first person she met among the Brethren. In those first foggy days after she came from the Tree, he nursed her back to health in his own bed, made her drink strong, sweet tea whose taste she now recalled with a hateful fondness. He fed her plates of roasted breadfruit and grilled tuna, doing everything in a silence she found disconcerting at first, but later learned to love. She could still remember his first words, spoken with an expression so certain it might have been carved in granite since the beginning of time:

"You come to a sad place."

The king visited her bedside—she did not find out until later what a remarkable boon this was. He stood looking down at her with his riot of hair and his broken features and his calm, dead eyes, and her first thought was that somehow she should know his name.

"She isn't fat enough," he said, looking at her but speaking to Disagree. "Perhaps a few sweets, some nougat."

"I don't know how," Disagree replied.

The king turned his head towards him, eyebrows raised.

"My maman always make it for me," Disagree said in self-defense.

"Then get Bessie, down the road, to make some. Feed her up. I don't want anyone to think I starved this one."

In the following months, she often wondered why he had chosen to favor her when he ignored all the other "new fish." She had found no satisfactory explanation until recently, the night he proposed her mission. And then he had sent Dis to help her escape from the Cyclops. *Why? It must have been because of what Dis said: You are a great treasure to him.*

Every day, she replayed the same sequence of memories until she came to an inescapable conclusion: The king must have chosen her from the beginning. After all, it stood to reason. Everyone said the king had sold his soul to gain Djinn powers. Perhaps he had the power to foretell the future . . . *Rise to the heights,* he said. And the more she thought about it, the more intensely burned the icy flame within her. Perhaps she would be the first queen of the Brethren, no longer wandering among the shacks of the camp, watching the lights in the windows and listening to the families inside. She would sleep in her own house, and when she was present they would have to bow and call her "Your Majesty," and they would listen when she spoke.

After the sun went down, the nights came over suddenly and without warning. Stars pricked through in clusters. Bella traced the constellations with her finger: the Phoenix and the Crown, the Table Mountain, the Hare. Still thinking, she rearranged herself lengthwise in the hull, her head propped on a coconut just beneath the helm. The motion of the dugout and the heavy *whup-whup* of the lateen lulled her towards a sleep she knew would never quite come.

Oh, for some Claw, she thought. Then: *It's been a while since I thought about it.*

By now, she should have been twitching like a hanging man, as she had often done when the supply dried up. But, confronted by her new sense of purpose, her addiction uttered a wistful sigh and retreated, leaving her with the serene conviction that nothing could assail her destiny.

After moonrise, a sound like a handful of pebbles hitting the water disturbed her. An arc of fish fluttered overhead on wings that glittered faintly in the moonlight. One night, two of them misjudged their flight and dropped on top of her, knocking the wind out of her stomach and bruising her thigh. One flip-flopped, slipping out of her grasp when she got hold of it before leaping back into the water. The other she finally beat to death with a club she had found in the bottom of the hull. She roasted it wings and all for breakfast, on a fire of coconut husks.

A string of islands began to mark her course—bulbous coral

formations alternated with pillars and arches crowned with untidy vegetation. The waters turned pale blue and crystalline, and shoals of fish swarmed in the shallows, an explosion of color beneath her, so thick she could dip her hand in and flip one out whenever she was hungry. When the water grew shallower still, Bella released the lateen, allowing it to flap in the wind, while she stepped out knee-deep and waded up to explore the islands. But none of them grew fruit trees, and Bella sailed on, wondering how long the remaining supplies of coconuts would last.

A week later, she saw a cloud of terns wheeling and diving over a dark mound on the ocean, and her spirits rose. Where there were terns, there had to be water and perhaps some fruit. As she sailed in towards the island, the terns grew thicker, darting around so rapidly, she thought it was a miracle they did not collide. They rose continually from the surface of the island, spiraling up into a cloud about fifty feet above, while others descended from the cloud to fight for space among the hundreds of grey shrieking bodies nesting on top of one another, so dense the ground writhed and fluttered, as if the earth itself was made of terns.

Bella searched in vain for a change in the color of the water. She was going to run up directly onto the rocks. She released the lateen in anticipation, and the boat slowed. As the dugout approached the edge of the island, she waited for the grinding sound of a collision. Instead a flock of terns broke into the air, and where a beach or a line of rocks should be, there was nothing but a loose tangle of twigs on the water. As she pushed on, terns rose in waves, revealing more water in place of land. Then the whole flock rose up in a thunder of shrieks and flutters, raining droppings, loose twigs, leaves, and broken eggs, and Bella found herself sitting in the midst of a mass of dead terns and branches that had formed a floating platform for the rest of the colony, which now circled above, turning afternoon to dusk.

The dugout came to a stop. Confronted with the sea of bodies, she was overcome by a sudden sense of futility.

Perhaps I should just go back, she thought. *It would be all right, just like he said.*

Then she shook her head. *No. I won't go back to "I told you so!"*

She pulled in the mainsheet and slowly worked the dugout through the miniature sea of frail corpses and tangled vegetation. On the other side, she corrected her course by the setting sun.

A day beyond the illusory island of birds, a more promising prospect appeared on the horizon—an island indented at the base, the top of which sprouted a grove of coconut trees. There was no reef. Deep water went right up to the island, where a narrow fringe of sand met the waves.

As Bella approached, the shape of the island blurred in her vision, and she shook her head, thinking she might have had too much sun. But the island continued to shake, growing more agitated. Now it was lifting at one end, revealing a cave from which a wrinkled head emerged on a neck that stretched on and on, so that Bella had to angle the dugout to port to avoid it.

Then flippers slid out from either side of the island, and she knew she was not looking at an island at all.

The giant turtle turned its head slowly to watch her pass, its eyes milky and expressionless with age.

"Have you seen my daughter?" it croaked.

"No, I haven't," Bella replied, ready to bear away if the turtle snapped at her.

"I'm been waiting here," the turtle said. "My little Tala—"

Keep her talking. "She was supposed to come?"

"She said she would meet Qatala. She promise. That's gratitude for you. Children, they are always so ungrateful." Qatala regarded Bella accusingly, as if she expected her to explain herself.

Bella looked at the sail, spilling the wind. "Some parents deserve it."

"Ha!" the turtle crowed. "Qatala know you'd say that. Little Tala always like that, always answer back, always think she know every-thing better. You probably the same way with your *maman*."

The dugout was slowing. Bella glanced up at the trees on Qatala's shell. She thought she could make out a banana tree in the tangle of the coconut grove. *A fresh banana . . .* Her mouth watered.

She turned back to the turtle. "I don't have a *maman*."

Qatala tilted her head and blinked slowly.

"At her age, dearie," she said slowly, "Qatala know all the lies ever told. You run away. Is Qatala right?"

Bella did not answer.

Qatala nodded with satisfaction. "That's why you're so thin. Your *maman* is waiting for you with food, but you don't want that, do you? You want some other food, something sweet, eh?"

"I'm hungry now," Bella cut in.

"No, no no," Qatala cackled. "Qatala is not finished yet. First you tell her why you run away, hmm?"

"I don't want to talk about it," Bella replied. She grasped the helm and began winding in the mainsheet, the sail filling. "And if you won't stop nosing into my private business, I can leave!"

"Just like my Tala, so sensitive!" Qatala slapped her flippers down, rocking the dugout. "It must be a sad thing. Why not come and sit down a little bit, and then you can run some more after that?"

Relieved, Bella stopped winding the mainsheet. She looked back at the turtle. "Are you going to leave me alone?"

Qatala rocked her head. "Qatala will take a little sleep while she waits for her Tala. Four or five days."

Bella hesitated for an appropriate length, then pushed away on the helm. The dugout eased around, slowing. With the last of its momentum, it came to ground on the sand in the lee of the tur-tle's body. Bella leapt out and made the boat fast on what appeared to be a root jutting from the vegetation that grew over the shell. Qatala craned her head to watch Bella pull herself upwards from handhold to foothold until she reached the clump of trees at the top. The turtle clucked in disapproval. "You climb like a monkey!"

Bella ignored her and began exploring the grove. She had been right—a large banana tree nestled among the coconut palms. The ground was thick with overripe fruit that squished under her feet. Bella used a fallen coconut to knock a bunch to the ground, only to discover a robber crab clinging to the stem. She tapped its carapace with a twig and when it grabbed, she tossed it gently out of the way before settling herself to eat. Bananas, the dullest staple of her life until now, had never tasted so delicious.

"Bonne nuit!" Qatala called from below. Bella mumbled a reply with her mouth full, and then there was silence. Presumably the turtle had retreated into her shell. Slowly, Bella ate the entire bunch, looking out over the sea. Clouds had suddenly blanketed the sky, turning the water a metallic grey that glittered in spots where beams of sunlight broke through the cover. She wondered vaguely if a storm was coming, but didn't give it much thought. Besides, she could hardly think of a safer place to weather a storm than on top of Qatala.

Her eyes drooped into half-sleep.

She started awake suddenly with the impression that the world had tilted under her. She sat up. The robber crab stood a few feet away, waving its claw as if trying to get her attention. The wind in her face possessed a cool urgency now. The ocean had faded to a dull grey, breaking out with whitecaps. Clouds rolled overhead, not even a patch of brightness to betray the sun.

Again the ground beneath her shifted, and Bella scrambled to her feet, clutching at the coconut tree beside her. She worked her way forward over the uneven tangle of vegetation to the front of the turtle's shell. Qatala had emerged and was regarding the rising storm with indifference.

With surprising energy, the turtle twisted her head to look up at Bella.

"Who are you?"

Bella blinked. Qatala's voice had changed—it was now younger, high and demanding, almost peevish.

"I—" she began. "I came in the boat—"

"Where's my mother?"

Bella found herself at a loss for words.

"Aren't you," she managed finally. "Weren't you looking for your daughter?"

"What daughter?"

"You said you were looking for Tala . . ."

"Don't be stupid," snapped the turtle. "*I'm* Tala. My mother wandered off yesterday. She hasn't been back since."

Bella was nonplussed. *She's crazy,* she thought. *A crazy turtle... Or maybe I'm the one who's crazy.*

"What are you doing on my back?" Tala demanded.

"You—that is, your mother said I could come and rest here…"

"Liar! I think I know my mother. Selfish old hag wouldn't give a barnacle a place to lodge if she could help it."

"But she did."

"You're not going to tell me you know my mother better than I do, are you?"

That's for certain, Bella thought. "No," she said.

"Of course not! And I'm telling you she wouldn't let just anyone on her precious shell. Even when I was a baby she wouldn't carry me. Truth is, you're an interloper. Trespassing in my space!"

"No, no," Bella protested. She craned to see the dugout, but could see nothing from this angle.

"Get off!" Tala shouted. "Interloper!" She bent her head and the shell rocked violently, throwing Bella off her feet. She began to slip off, but immediately grabbed at a root and steadied herself.

Tala peered up at her malevolently.

"Still sticking, eh?" she screeched. "Not an interloper at all, are you? You're a leech, a filthy parasite!"

"I swear, your mother invited me!" Bella shouted.

"Well, I'm *un*inviting you!"

"All right, I'm going. Just let me get to my boat!"

"You have one minute, parasite," Tala replied. "Then I go under and you can make your own island."

Bella looked into the impenetrable depths of the water around her. The sandbar around the turtle had sunk underwater. The waves exploded directly against the shell. The wind was a solid thing, pushing into her face. Fear fluttered in her heart and she scrambled back along the shell. The dugout was still nowhere to be seen, and a premonition of disaster overtook her.

At last, she stopped at the place where she had tied up, and stared at the frayed end of the rope in the muddy water that swirled among the loose earth and vegetation at the base of the shell.

Tala's head appeared from around the curve of the shell. "Are you still here?"

"Listen, Tala," Bella began, holding out her hand. "My boat got—"

"Your problem," Tala cut in. "Goodbye, little parasite."

"No!" Bella shouted. But the turtle was already pushing herself forward as the trees on her shell thrashed. It was raining now. Colder than the usual afternoon showers, the drops stung her skin like stones. The wind rushed over the water, blowing foam off the whitecaps. It was a monsoon squall, and good as she was in water, Bella knew she stood no chance in this weather.

"Please stop!" Bella entreated. Tala ignored her, dragging her body half into the water. The first waves exploded over her head. Bella scrambled upwards, pursued by the water. Tala was swimming. The vegetation on her carapace shifted and slid off, revealing the regular patterns beneath.

Bella reached the top of the shell just ahead of the water. The wind had shaken the palm trees bare of all their nuts and stripped the banana trees of their leaves. Crabs scuttled back and forth, waving their claws, panic-stricken as they sought a way out. But it was inexorable: Tala's powerful fins paddled her forward into the waves, all the time descending beneath the surface.

Water rushed over Bella's feet and then rose to her knees. Overhead, the coconut trees lost their hold on the earth, shifted and slowly toppled over, exploding the surface as they hit, their roots clawing at the sky. Without hesitating, Bella gathered herself and leapt, landing on one of the trunks to watch as the rest of the turtle island went under. Nothing but a few tangled twigs marked the place where Tala had been, soon churned up by the thrashing waves.

After that, the world disintegrated into a mass of wind and water. Water forced itself down Bella's throat, up her nose and into her eyes, blinding her with salt. Wind choked her with its force. The trunk to which she clung whipped back and forward, battering her chest so hard that she wept at the pain, at one moment diving, at another tossing and spinning, defying her to hold on. The flesh on her hands softened, then tore and bled. Her nails ripped.

Minutes coalesced into hours, then slowed into minutes again. She felt her grip loosening. Just before she let go, she thought about Dis, and the sadness returned—the sadness she knew whenever the Claw began to take hold of her. Suddenly, a memory of the time before the Tree returned. Qatala had been right—she had run away one night and now she could not go back. The sadness rose higher, covering her head like the waves. She wanted nothing but to let go. So at last she did, pulled instantly under by the waves. For a brief moment, she resurfaced, saw a break in the clouds and beam of light playing on the surface. *The storm must be over*, she thought. And she went under again. Water flooded her mouth and nose and burned in her throat. She choked, sinking faster with her legs and arms twitching.

The last thing she felt was someone embracing her and pressing lips on hers.

And then she died.

LETHES II

onah Comfait turned off the sea road onto the road that climbed up towards the mountain. Actually, it was not so much a road as a couple of parallel mud tracks, between which the grass grew almost knee-high. On either side, bushes and thorny vines threatened to overwhelm any sign of the tracks. Trees closed overhead, sealing in the heat of the morning.

The forest gave way to a clearing where the Morgans' house slumped, decaying on its stilts. Surrounding the building and in the spaces beneath the stilts lay the rusted parts of old cars, while further out in the yard entire wrecks sank into untended vegetation. Bred from stagnant pools, the mosquitoes were almost unbearable, hanging in visible clouds over the place and descending thickly onto Jonah's skin in spite of his best efforts to sweep them off.

A large dog with its fur falling off in patches rushed out, barking and snarling. Having suffered a bite on his first visit, Jonah did not attempt to be friendly, but kicked the animal soundly as it leaped at him. The dog fell back yelping, and then ran off with its tail between its legs.

A woman stood in the open doorway. She was short, skinny, with a dried appearance and cropped crimson hair that had obviously been dyed—and some time ago. The grey-blond roots showed clearly.

"So you came, eh?" she called in the gravelly voice of a heavy smoker. "Don't know why you bothered, *mon boy*. She's not worth it, is what I say. But you might as well come in, now you're here."

As he stepped inside, Charlene Morgan was already seated at the dining table, with the half-smoked cigarette she had abandoned a few minutes earlier pinched at the tips of her fingers. Clouds of smoke hung about prematurely aged features. She gestured Jonah to the chair opposite.

"We're sick and tired of this, Jonah!" she said.

Jonah sat down at the table. Overflowing ashtrays and dirty cutlery cluttered the surface. Every clear area was sticky. The rest of the room was no better—the floors stained and dirty, and the lime green furniture, plastic-covered, featured burn marks where careless cigarettes had rested. Large holes pockmarked the window netting, useless to resist mosquitoes that swarmed as thickly inside as out, and once again, Jonah experienced the impression that the Morgans had been squatting in someone else's abandoned home for the last twenty years.

From the far side of the room, Ray Morgan echoed his wife. "As the woman says, we're tired, my boy. Tired of trying with her." Slouched in an armchair beside a vase of dusty artificial roses, Isabella's father wore a pair of filthy underwear. He was all grime and flab and wrinkles, the only clean spot being a bandaged patch on the left side of his chest. Under a tangle of dirty-sand hair that reminded Jonah of Isabella, Ray's dull grey eyes registered a permanent expression of surprise, as if he could not quite comprehend why he had been dealt such a hand. Stimulated by the morning heat, rivulets of sweat were already streaking his forehead.

"We give that girl everything," Ray declared. "Everything she wants, we give it to her if we can. Money, everything."

Everything but what she needs, Jonah thought.

"As a matter of fact," Charlene said, "that's what happened last night. She comes in with that face on—you know the one. She doesn't want to eat, just money she wants. More money from what

I give her yesterday. I say no, because I know she give it to that lay-about Maxim up at Anse Aux Pins. I tell her if she wants cigarettes I have some. But no, just money. I say no again and she starts screaming and throwing things like she always does. She gets so worked up by then that she goes to her room and she won't come out. What can I do?"

Charlene looked at Jonah as if he might know the answer. Seeing none in his face, she continued. "Then this one comes home," she jerked her head at Ray, "and he throws a nonsense. As if he could do any better!" She jabbed the tip of her cigarette at her husband. "He can judge! He barely sees her, barely talks to her. And then he comes in like he'll fix everything. Pah!" She spat and leaned back in her chair, shrouding her anger in an exhalation of smoke.

"Let me tell you something, *mon boy*," Ray murmured, examining his bandaged side. "Let me tell you something about women. They whine about independence and freedom. And when you give it to them and it all falls to hell—of course it does!—all of a sudden it's your fault. You're this, you're that. And then they want you to pick up the pieces for them! It never fails, I tell you! I don't know how many times—" his voice rose now— "we talk about this. No more money until she respect us! And then I come home," he bellowed, "and I find she trying it again! So I go to try and calm the girl down, you see. I try to talk some sense, just to put a little scare in her. Nothing rough. And you know what that little hussy does?"

Jonah just looked at him. He felt like he was swimming in sewage.

"She stab me!" Ray paused to let the outrageousness of it register. "And while I'm on the bed bleeding, she's out the door and off running. Can you believe that?" he looked at Jonah expectantly.

Jonah was silent, looking at the floor.

"Her own father," Ray persisted. "She almost kill me."

"Did she?" Jonah asked.

"Ah!" Charlene exclaimed. "Just a scratch on his ribs. He's such a baby!"

"I tell you, I'm sick of it!" Ray shouted. "She cross a line there!"

"Well, what do you want me to do about it?" Charlene muttered. "Nothing I do is good enough for you!"

"Call that sister of yours," Ray replied. "She wants to take Isabella off our hands. She can have her now!"

Charlene said nothing.

"Call her!" Ray repeated.

Charlene looked at him with a poisonous expression. "I won't," she hissed. "I won't go to her with my hat in my hands. I'm sorry, my dear Marie-Therese," her voice became a parody, "you and your high and mighty morals were right—I'm just not fit to be a mother! Here, have my daughter. Have her baptized by a priest, make her into another self-righteous *couyon** . . ."

"I don't care," Ray shot back. "Maybe she can teach the girl some morals for a change. Call her, Charlene!"

"No!"

Ray leaned forward aggressively. "Then I will."

"Do that and you can kiss me goodbye too!" Charlene flicked the burning stub of her cigarette at him. He dodged and it hit the back of his chair, adding another burn mark before dropping out of sight.

"So this is what you want?" he cried, spreading his arms. "More of this until she's eighteen? And you think she's gone then? I bet you anything you want she goes and gets herself pregnant and then we have to take care of her and some layabout's little *batarde*. For the rest of our lives? No." He shook his head and looked at Jonah. "We deserve our rest, Jonah. It's our turn now!"

"I can't go to her." Charlene's voice was weaker now, crumbling. "My hat in my hands to Her Highness."

"You don't need to, I tell you," Ray said. "I call, I explain everything. Just a while until she straightens up."

Charlene was silent.

Jonah stood, feeling vaguely nauseous. "I suppose I should go then," he said. "I have some . . . studying."

"I'm sorry to bring you out," Charlene peered up at him through her smoke. "Here." She fumbled around on the cluttered table until she found a few crumpled notes and offered them to him.

"No, it's fine," Jonah said. "When we've had a lesson I'll take it."

Charlene sighed. "Well, I don't know about these lessons anymore." She glanced at Ray resentfully.

"Really, it's fine," Jonah said. "Just let me know when it's a good day."

Ray snorted. "Good day! I don't remember the last good day!"

Jonah shrugged.

"We call you," Charlene said, almost friendly. "Thank you, Jonah."

"*Oui,*" Ray muttered, stroking his bandaged side. "Thanks, *mon boy.*"

Jonah stumbled down the steps and walked quickly away. The dog growled from under the house and, when Jonah was a little further away, ventured a bark. But the fight was long gone out of him, and he made no attempt to follow. As the squalor of the Morgan property sank mercifully behind the impenetrable tangle of forest, the nausea in Jonah's gut slowly faded.

He could not count how many times he had arrived to give Isabella her lesson only to find she had run away. On other occasions, he had found her curled up on the floor by her bed, her tangle of blond hair filthy and unwashed. She had not even spoken to him then. And when he managed to coax her upright and tried to get her to start a worksheet, she responded with sarcasm and monosyllables. He had been forced to spend many of their sessions just finding out what was wrong. Sometimes Jonah thought that helped. Isabella had spoken about how much she hated her parents, especially her father.

"He's a pig," she said, staring ahead while she chewed on her nails.

These conversations made her temporarily amenable to a lesson, but she soon lapsed into sullenness, which degenerated into tears and tantrums when her mother tried to make her cooperate.

And there was his attempt to tell her about Mysterion. She said, "My dad says only fools and weaklings like her believe in anything other than what's in front of them." Facing her implacable derision, he had given up, overwhelmed by the sense of his own inadequacy.

Several yards before he reached the sea road, he turned right onto a barely visible path in the undergrowth and followed it back towards the mountain. He was skirting the edge of the Morgan property, though the house never became visible among the trees. As the path climbed, it vanished sporadically, sinking into pools, stagnant and mosquito-infested. Jonah stepped over them without hesitation. He knew exactly where he was going; he and Isabella had taken this path more than once, during the many extended breaks between his attempts at teaching.

She revealed this place to him one day during an unusual bout of clarity and coherence. When he would have continued along the path towards the boutiques where she would buy cigarettes—her usual habit during the breaks—she jerked her head and turned to follow this path. He asked her where they were going, and she smiled with a joy that shocked him.

"A secret place," she said. "Where I talk to the dead."

Vague and fitful before, the path now vanished entirely. Jonah did not hesitate, recognizing the markers from the previous times: the heart-shaped rock on the right, the bent-old-man jackfruit tree to the left. The bushes coated him with cobwebs as they parted to let him pass. Ahead, the graveyard lay as if frozen in its own time. Morning sunlight streamed down through the trees. At the far edge, still sunk in shadows, was the place where she had often taken him.

Isabella was sitting there now, her knees pulled up into the fetal position Jonah knew so well, while her sleeping face, cold and set and pale, seemed a mere extrusion of the gravestone at her back.

CHAPTER TWELVE
𝔸N ESCORT OF MERMAIDS

So it's true—death doesn't stop your thoughts. How disappointing. Then Bella became conscious of moving through water. She lay horizontally, facing downward, her arms pressed to her sides and legs together, like a submarine sarcophagus flying through the darkness.

Are you Isabella Morgan?

A woman's voice had spoken into her head. Fighting whatever bound her limbs, struggling to control the chaos of her heartbeats, Bella tried to reply. No sound emerged. Water flowed easily into her throat and lungs, and she knew she was not breathing air.

Am I really dead? she thought.

The response came: *We decide that. Are you Isabella Morgan?*

The voice belonged to a young woman—cheerful, matter-of-fact. Bella thrashed and shook her head.

That's not my name.

Anymore, you mean.

What?

It's not your name anymore.

Bella twisted her head around in terror. The darkness pressed into her vision.

My mother gave me my name. It reminds me of her—Cybele, she always said, swim close to me, it's dangerous.

Where are you?

I am close.

I can't see you.

It's night. But if you look from where we came, you can see our wake. Bella twisted her head over her shoulder and saw phosphorescent streams spiraling away from her.

The voice resounded in her head again: *Is that why you don't want that name?*

I don't understand. Who are you?

Because you don't want to remember that they gave it to you?

Am I dead?

We decide that.

When? Where are we going?

No fretting about it. You will see when we arrive.

I can't move!

No, you can't. We bound you for the journey.

Where? Bella screamed inside her head. *Where are we going?*

Shh. Calm yourself, my love.

Bella struggled and contorted in fury, but her limbs stuck fast. She opened her mouth and screamed with all her strength. The sound resonated in her imagination. At last, she subsided, her lungs heaving in slow motion. This must be her captor's magic. She wasn't dead, just bewitched.

With a great effort, she regained control of herself and forced her limbs to relax. After a minute of concentration with her eyes closed, her breaths slowed. Her mind acquired an unnatural calm. *If she asked me about that name, she was expecting me . . . How did they know? But that doesn't matter, stupid. Just like Dis said, Crato must have warned them and they were waiting. But not to kill me. As a prisoner I'm more valuable . . .*

She opened her eyes and spoke a thought: *My name is Isabella Morgan.*

Good. Bella could almost hear the person smile. *I knew it somehow.*

How did you know?

I don't know . . . The voice sounded vague. *Perhaps you just look like it.*

Are you joking? Bella thought. *And how's an Isabella supposed to look?*

Not an ordinary Isabella. Just a pirate one.

Oh, I see. Bella felt her fury rising. *And how's a pirate Isabella supposed to look?*

Like a wild thing. Tangled hair. Just like you.

You know lots of pirates named Isabella who look like that?

Not really. Just you.

So you knew I was Isabella because you knew what I looked like.

Perhaps. The Elder showed you in our Seeing Pool.

And how did he know me?

He didn't say.

So I'm not going to die, then.

The voice was smiling again. *We're all going to die, my dear. At least until the Higher Mysterion comes.*

Now, I mean!

Well, you're not dead now, no.

Bella gritted her teeth in frustration. *I mean, you don't want to kill me.*

Oh dear, no. We don't do that.

So what do *you do?*

We bring back the dead. Or we leave them as they are.

So you brought me back. Where are you taking me? To this Elder person?

You'll see, my love. A hand stroked Bella's cheek. She jerked away.

Poor thing, the voice said. *You aren't used to that, are you?*

Leave me alone. Just tell me where you're taking me!

As I said, the voice murmured, *you will see. Until then, why don't you just enjoy the journey, hmm?*

A Djinn's fart on that.

Well, then, perhaps we should talk again when you're a little happier.

Whatever you say.

The presence in the voice retreated from Bella's mind. The hole of silence amplified the beating of her heart.

The darkness was no longer a solid thing. Bella could tell distances within the void. The first light reached down and lit up tinges of green and blue. Then she saw them—a group of six mermaids gliding beside her. Three younger ones wore their hair arranged in elaborate spirals and giggled at one another in unspoken gossip. The two elders allowed their unbound hair to trail behind them and looked as if nothing could surprise them. Swimming closest was the mermaid Bella instinctively knew was the leader, probably the one who had spoken in her mind. She was older than Bella had imagined, with an ugly, pleasant face and hair plaited into two long ropes that trailed all the way down to her tail—that of a giant angelfish.

The mermaid looked down and met Bella's eyes. She smiled politely, but her presence did not enter Bella's mind, as it had earlier. That distancing bothered Bella, but she steeled herself to meet the mermaid's smile with unflinching defiance. The mermaid's smile grew ironic, as if she were aware of Bella's struggle, just before she turned her attention back to the course.

Only then did Bella realize that none of her escorts were holding her by a chain or a rope. She was simply floating between them, moving in exact coordination with their movements. She had been right, she realized—she was enchanted, and no amount of effort would be able to free her.

The light falling from the surface strengthened. Outlines of distant masses rose out of the green haze. As they swam closer, the shapes resolved into immense coral structures—towers and walls around which swarmed shoals of fish like underwater birds, rising, circling, and roosting.

They swept through coral mountains and over valleys. Then they broke out onto a great plain. Shipwrecks littered the sand as far as she could see. There were ships she knew—schooners and frigates and square-riggers and dhows—and others she could not recognize—odd, cylindrical shapes with round sails that looked as if they had been fashioned in an age yet to come.

The mermaids swerved through the maze of hulls and broken yards at a terrifying speed. They narrowly dodged the jagged edges and obstacles that rushed past, without a break in their tranquility.

Bella looked up at the leader. *Where did the ships come from?*

The leader smiled. *Calmed down a little, have we?*

Bella shrugged. *What choice do I have?*

That's the spirit. My name is Cybele.

The voices of the other mermaids crowded one after another:

I am Coenobia.

Astarsha.

Eo.

I'm Ruzhivo.

Lac.

You asked about the ships, Cybele said. Bella nodded. *They come from a great battle of Mysterion long ago.*

Who fought? The Brethren?

No, this was before the Brethren. A battle between the People of the Wind and those who served the Djinn.

Who won?

The Djinn, at first. Then Tinashe gave herself up, and later, Monvieil rose up and defeated the Djinn.

Tinashe. She had never heard the name before. *But Monvieil is gone now.*

Cybele looked at her. *Yes.*

And the Elder is their leader now?

Cybele tilted her head. *Why do you ask about things you already know?*

Bella felt her face grow warm in spite of the cool water. They were past the ships now, sweeping over the open plain. It was bare here, except for patches of seaweed waving in the current and great shoals of angelfish and parrotfish moving in unison in the distance. Looking closer, Bella made out larger fish-shapes moving at the edges of the shoals. Were they sharks?

So why are you here? Cybele asked. *A one-girl pirate invasion from the West?*

Bella was silent. Perhaps it was best not to say anything.

I'm just teasing, Cybele went on. *I know this was a difficult thing to do.*

Bella felt relieved. *You're not making it any easier.*

I'm sorry, my love, Cybele said. *But we mermaids have a saying: Love a Djinn before you trust a pirate.*

I left the pirates.

Ah, but you see, that has yet to be seen.

Ahead, the shoals converged. The creatures she had thought were sharks were actually mermaids. Each held a net between two sticks as they drove the fish into a single swirling mass.

Bella decided to change the subject. *Catching a little dinner?* She gestured to the shoal with her chin.

They are not for us, Cybele replied. *We're taking them to the fishermen.*

A younger mermaid, the one named Eo, chimed in with a giggle: *And they think they do all the hard work.*

Each to her own, the elder named Coenobia replied.

Each to her own, Astarsha echoed.

That may be so, my ladies, Lac chimed in, *but have you tried herding those slippery little buggers?*

Yah, Ruzhivo cried. *Talk about work!*

We did it for a hundred and twenty-two years, Coenobia replied frostily.

A hundred and twenty-two years. Astarsha nodded.

So I think I know what it was like, Coenobia finished.

The young mermaids fell silent, momentarily cowed.

Cybele broke the silence. *Over there the shallows begin.*

She pointed to where the plains ended and a flat-topped range of mountains spread across the ocean floor as far as Bella could see. The herders were driving the shoal forward now, following the same course as Bella and her escorts. At their speed, the range closed rapidly, looming higher until Bella could no longer see the tops. In some places, the cliffs jutted out, a maze of coral matted with seaweed and swarming with sea life. Then the walls receded into inlets whose depths were lost in darkness. The herders drove straight for the largest of these gaps.

Bella spoke: *You're taking me to the People of the Wind.*

Patience, Cybele replied.

As they entered the inlet, darkness closed around Bella again, concealing her escort. They swam along in silence. Finally, Bella felt herself slowing until the water no longer flowed on her skin.

Where are we?

No answer. The silence pushed in on her. The presence of the mermaids around her had receded, and fear gripped her chest. In spite of the futility of it, she began to struggle against whatever bound her. To her surprise, her limbs came apart. She was free, her clothes floating around her.

Then the dark water began to flutter. Hundreds of currents beat against her skin. Bella froze, terrified.

What's happening? But even as she spoke, the words flowing past her lips turned to salt. Seawater raked her lungs. She clawed the water around her, kicking as the sensation of drowning overtook her.

A voice, Cybele's, spoke in her head with a new authority: *What do you want with us, Isabella Morgan?*

Bella shuddered but did not reply.

Tell me what you want!

Dying. Isabella choked out the word, her consciousness flickering.

You have been dead for years. Do you want to live?

Yes.

Then you have your life for now. Remember the gift and rise up!

In unison, the mermaids started singing in the darkness. A strange wordless melody filled Bella's head, high and discordant with a drone in place of a harmony. A sudden rush of small bodies pressed against her, finning frantically away from the mermaid's song, bearing her upward. *Fish.* She could see the surface now, ripples highlighted in the blue morning sky beyond. The narrow shapes of boats formed in a rough circle and heads peered over the gunwales.

She rose past the lower edge of the nets, buffeted in the storm of angelfish and bluefish and red snappers. She broke the surface in a crush of bodies that drove into her from every direction. Hands lifted her out as water spewed from her mouth and nose, and her breath flooded fire in her lungs.

CHAPTER THIRTEEN
PLAYING HORSEY

When her coughing eased, she opened her eyes, only to narrow them immediately against the sun. She lay on a bundle of nets at the bottom of a boat. Around and above, voices tumbled over one another.

"I haven't seen one of them come back since—"

"Sartish. It was Sartish, the last one."

"No, no. Surely—"

"It was Sartish, I tell you!"

"She's too thin, this one."

"Too thin, too fat. Is that all you think about, Magritte?"

"Uh, Dio, are you going to be giving out fish any time?"

"They should bring her to my house. I'd fatten her up with some nice *la daube.**"

"They won't bring her to your place! If she goes anywhere, they'll take her to him, *sous le montaigne.**"

"That red snapper there looks good. Dio, could you possibly . . . ?"

"In a moment, *madame*. Someone's gone to the New Elder."

Jonah, Bella thought sluggishly, and rolled her eyes upward. Several women stared down at her. Some had skin like new charcoal and green eyes, others had Asiatic eyes and skin the color of coffee with cream; and there were mulatto women with red hair and blue eyes. They all wore cotton dresses printed with lilies, orchids, and vines on sky-blue or sun-yellow backgrounds. A black man with a heavy pleasant face bent over her.

"Well, hello there," he said, smiling. He spoke very slowly, with a touch of a slur at the edge of his words.

"Michel, didn't I say stay back?" Bella turned towards the voice—a pale man with sharp features.

Michel's face fell. "Sorry, Dio," he said. "I just wanted to say hello."

"*Love a Djinn before you trust a pirate.* While you're saying hello, she could stick a knife between your ribs."

"Oh," Michel said. He looked down at Bella. "She doesn't look dangerous. She looks lost, that's all."

Bella's hackles rose. She tried to rise. Her muscles screamed and she sank down. Whatever magic the mermaids had used to bind her had also served to numb her body. Now she remembered the wounds from the storm—the bruises on her chest and her finger-nails torn to the quick.

Michel had backed away at her movement.

"Just leave her, I tell you!"

"All right, Dio." Michel sat beside Dio on the gunwale.

"Don't move, *mam'zelle*," Dio warned Bella. "You're not going anywhere anyway without a guard."

Bella spoke through her pain. "I thought the People of the Wind were supposed to be hospitable . . . to strangers."

"Hospitable, yes. Not a bunch of *couyons*."

"So I'm a prisoner then."

"Not exactly," Dio grinned. "You can't trust anyone these days. Let's just say you're on probation."

Silence fell as the people stared at Bella. Dio had inspired them—she could see a new fear in their eyes.

Suddenly, she remembered something and reached up to her throat. At first she could not feel the cord and panicked. Then— there it was. She slipped the doubloon back into place.

Dio grinned. "What you were looking for, *mam'zelle?*"

Bella said nothing.

"Don't worry," Dio said. "We didn't touch your little necklace."

"I know," Bella croaked. "You'd be missing some fingers if you did."

Dio grinned wider and opened his mouth to reply.

"There they are," one of the women said.

The others turned. Bella dared not move.

Dio addressed someone outside her line of sight. "Found her in the nets this morning."

A head appeared over the edge of the gunwale. He was a boy her age, perhaps a little older. He had dark skin and roughly carved features. His black eyes glittered like lumps of newly washed coal.

"You are calling yourself . . ." The boy's accent reminded Bella of Apoojamy, but not as pronounced.

"Bella Couteau," she replied, meeting his eyes directly.

"And the name you left in the Tree?"

He knows about the leaving of names. He was one of us! "Isabella Morgan," she said reluctantly.

The boy glanced behind him and nodded to someone out of Bella's sight.

"It's her," he said.

They know! It's over.

The boy turned back. "I am Sartish," he said abruptly.

Hodoul's ward, the one who ran away!

"I . . . I thought you died," she said.

Sartish smiled—a sharp, lopsided grin. "That is the story they relate. Are you capable of getting up unaided?"

Bella tried to push herself upright again, and gasped.

"Are you requiring some assistance?" Sartish said.

"No," Bella grunted, and tried again.

Sartish glanced behind him again and gestured. "Azrel, provide her assistance."

"I'm fine," Bella insisted. Her eyes had filled with tears at the pain.

"You are wasting time," Sartish replied. Then the Azrel he had addressed appeared, and Bella fell back, overcome by the vision of the creature who rose above her against the sky. From the descriptions of those who had seen one, she recognized an Angelus—*a creature of wings and light*, they said. She had not believed them. And yet, here it was. Long wings entwined to formed the semblance of limbs; tiny wings nestled around a body; wings blew around its head like locks of hair. And always light fluttering everywhere. Only the Angelus's face was flesh—a full heart shape, with a sarcastic mouth and bright green eyes mocking Bella.

"It's my lot in life," Azrel remarked. "Carrying humans who can't seem to stand on their own two feet."

"I can stand just fine," Bella replied. She began struggling again.

"Unlikely," Sartish said. "Take her, Azrel. The Elder is waiting for us."

"Then she needs to hold still and let me do it," Azrel snapped.

"Cease your struggling," Sartish said to Bella. "Immediately."

Bella ignored them both and pushed herself further upright as the pain threatened to black out her vision.

Sartish grabbed her throat. "Desist." Bella choked and dropped back into a prone position. She fumbled, trying to break his grip, but his hand seemed to have been carved onto her neck. Irrelevantly, she noticed that his forearms were covered with small pockmarks. Still struggling, she reached down to where she had hidden her switchblade. It was gone.

"This is what you're looking for?" Dio proudly displayed the blade in his hands.

"First thing we take," Sartish grinned coldly at her. "I know how it works."

"Let go," she gasped.

"Stop then."

Bella relaxed her struggles. Sartish let go. As Bella coughed to regain her breathing, Azrel pulled her up onto her back. Bella squirmed, disturbed by the sensation that she had fallen into a nest of birds. Azrel rose above the crowd. In either direction, the beach stretched white and blinding until it curved out of sight. Green waves rolled off the open ocean. With Sartish following, Azrel floated towards the head of the beach where the island rose up in a wall of coconut and mangrove trees. The crowd watched their progress, then turned back to the forgotten catch, haggling over who would get what, with Dio acting as mediator.

"Joe would love a nice red snapper for dinner, cooked with chilies."

"If it's not too much trouble, I'll take that tuna. That one there."

"But he's only one man. I have five children to feed!"

"Would you please make up your minds. Some of us have things to do!"

"Dio, you decide."

"Well," Dio began portentously. "In my opinion . . ."

But the rest of Dio's opinion was lost as the beach fell behind and the trees closed around them. No longer stirred by the onshore breeze, the air slowed to the consistency of heated oil. In the branches, myna birds squabbled over ripe jackfruit with shrieks that intensified the heat. Azrel floated above a narrow, beaten path between the trees. Bella was just wondering where Sartish had gotten to when she heard his voice, irritated and distant behind them:

"Slower, Azrel!"

Azrel sighed and slowed to a hover. "It seems a miracle to me," she said, "that human beings have intelligence enough to stand on two feet. How do you manage it? It must be like walking on stilts! A bit challenging for creatures of your level of intellectual development, if you ask me—"

"Didn't ask you," Sartish said, coming up beside them. His hair glistened and his dark face ran with sweat. "But I will be informing you of this much: the Wind made a mistake giving you a mouth."

"Well," Azrel replied, raising her eyebrows. "If you won't listen to the ageless wisdom of the Angeli—"

"Not that I will not—I'm having no choice, that's all."

Azrel's smile grew slightly provocative. "You can always go back to the pirates."

Sartish inclined his head. "Sometimes you make me think about it. So much for the wisdom of the Angeli."

Azrel struck her breast theatrically. "Ah, Sartish, you wound me! You don't really mean that, do you?"

"Want to test it?"

"Fine, Mister I-think-I-know-better-because-I've-seen-both-sides. Lead the way."

Sartish inclined his head. "At last, some true wisdom!" He grinned sharply at Bella and then strode ahead. Azrel followed behind. Occasionally, Bella heard her mutter things like, "Look at that—he just set a new record for all-time slowest land speed by a bipedal creature," and "If we were going any slower we'd be walking backwards." Sartish ignored these comments, though he occasionally flashed a grin back at them to indicate that he had heard.

The path threaded its way up through the forest, jogging at odd angles. At length, it cut a red earth road lined with almond and breadfruit trees, beyond which the forest continued inland. Along the road strolled women in bright dresses and men in slacks, bare-chested or wearing loose shirts. A string of children wound by, engaged in some imaginary quest. They alone seemed to have a purpose. Everyone else displayed an irritating lack of urgency, walking several yards before pausing to sit and chat, then rising to move on or turning back where they came from.

As they joined the stream of traffic, several people called greetings to Sartish, who, in spite of his haste (and much to Azrel's annoyance), paused to say hello. Some of them regarded Bella with pointed interest, and Sartish explained: "A refugee caught in the nets."

Impressed nods. "Really! What's her name?"

Sartish glanced at Bella and grinned out of the corner of his mouth. "You can call her Isabella."

More nods and smiles. "Welcome, welcome."

Bella barely nodded without meeting anyone's eyes. She felt awkward and ridiculous clinging to Azrel's back, a feeling that did nothing to ease her general sense of frustration. She had hoped to approach the island and accomplish her mission, after careful observation and reconnaissance, with forethought and stealth. But even before she laid eyes on the place, she had been taken captive and stripped of her weapon. And now she was being carried helplessly along in a pathetic procession, an object of curiosity for anyone with nothing better to do.

Sartish and Azrel moved on slowly, forced to conform to the pace of the crowd. At last, the road entered an open circle of sand that reminded Bella of the parlay square back at home. At points along the circumference, groups of people emerged from the trees. They abandoned all pretense at direction and settled into little groups in the shade. The sounds of their conversations in the air were soft, desultory. Occasional laughter broke out like birdcalls.

Watching Sartish make the round of greetings, Bella could not restrain herself. "What are they talking about?"

Azrel shrugged under her hands. "Nothing, really. The air, the fish, the color of the sunset, their dreams."

"What's the point?"

"No point. Just an excuse to hear each other's voices."

"They all know each other then?"

"There aren't that many—a few hundred. And they're probably all related!"

"Like one big happy family," Bella said sarcastically.

Azrel raised her eyebrows. "You don't like that?"

Bella smiled. "We're independent."

"You *were*."

"What?"

"You don't live that way anymore," Azrel said. "You live here with us now."

Bella did not answer, but shifted uncomfortably. Azrel's ceaseless fluttering was really bothering her.

Azrel addressed Sartish: "Can we move along, Sartish?"

"Fine, fine," Sartish snapped. "Nothing wrong with being polite." He led the way more quickly, calling and waving his greetings as they went. Above the trees, a mountain rose like the fin of a great sea creature, running in either direction as far as Bella could see. Sartish did not pause at the forest, but pushed on, finding a path among the fallen leaves and overgrown shrubs.

Another laughing, screaming line of children darted past and disappeared up the slope ahead. As Sartish, Azrel, and Bella followed, houses appeared. Small wooden bungalows with thatched roofs stood on carved stilts. Others were built around the trunks of trees, and still others were simple lean-tos with plank floors and walls made from billowing white curtains. Outside the houses, people sat in low chairs, sipping drinks and nibbling pieces of fruit. And again the muted, languorous voices rose in welcome as they passed. This time, though, Sartish did not stop to talk. He was caught up in the effort of the climb through the morning heat, which had descended with full force. Further up the slope, the houses grew less frequent until the forest was a solid, unbroken wall around them. Even the sound of birds squabbling faded to a complete silence that filled every space in Bella's hearing.

Yet another group of children rushed by them. Bella frowned.

"Where are they going?" she asked.

"Same place we are," Sartish grunted. He did not elaborate.

Several minutes later, the forest thinned and gave way to knee-high scrub and then to a granite plateau carpeted with moss and lichen. Clear of the trees, the wind buffeted Azrel as she followed Sartish along a narrow path that wound its way to the mountain peak in a nest of bright, tumbling clouds. The children vanished, but this time Bella kept hold of her curiosity.

While Azrel sighed and muttered, Sartish paused here and wiped his dripping forehead. Bella looked back. The canopy spread below, while in the distance, the ocean was an expanse of shattered reflections that darkened in patches as great, solitary clouds sailed above.

Sartish had pulled out a clear flask and was taking a long drink. He offered the flask to Bella. Thirst overcoming her hesitation, she took it without a word. The liquid was water, as fresh as citrus and surprisingly cool, as if it had just been taken from an underground stream. She drank her fill, and was surprised to find that the flask was no emptier than before.

"It was coming from above the heavens," Sartish explained.

"But why doesn't the water go down?" Bella asked, her curiosity forcing her.

"Don't know," Sartish said. "But I am certain it is not water. It is what our water comes from, or something."

Azrel sighed. "I've explained this to you *ad nauseam*, I think."

"Nausea is absolutely correct," Sartish muttered.

"Then perhaps you should listen for once," Azrel told him. "It is the *ideal* form of water," she explained to Bella. "It comes from the stream of Okean, and unlike water, it can never be consumed."

The stream of Okay-an . . . Bella was puzzled, but resisted the urge to ask. Her survival now depended on silence. How much did these people know about why she was really here? It might well be everything. Crato might or might not have told them about the Cyclops's death. Either way, if they succeeded in drawing her into conversation, they might lead her into further betrayals.

"Feel any better?" Azrel asked.

Bella realized her body no longer hurt. She flexed her limbs. *Good as new!* she thought. *I must get some of that water.*

"Can you walk?"

Bella nodded, glad to get out of her ridiculous position.

"Good." With relief, Azrel dropped her to the ground. "But I will ask you to walk ahead of me, please."

"So I *am* your prisoner," Bella said.

Azrel shrugged. "If that's how you want to think about it."

They continued up the mountain. Bella's muscles warmed quickly, and she kept pace with Sartish even on the steepest parts of the path, while Azrel floated behind them. The wind pushed and moaned from below, cooling the sweat on Bella's back.

Then, almost without warning, they stepped up into the cloud. The panorama of the island and the ocean was blotted out. A brilliant space opened up, where sunlight and wind mingled into bright banks and spirals and trails that gathered and circled endlessly. The air was cooler here, a relief from the solid heat below.

Sartish strode on ahead, unerring in his direction. Bella knew the peak must be close, but the cloud concealed everything, including the path beneath her feet. For all she knew, she could be walking on the edge of a cliff. One misstep and . . . The thought brought her to a halt. Her stomach fluttering, she looked for Azrel—the angelus was almost invisible, white on the white of cloud.

"Where are we going?" she called.

"Just follow," Azrel replied in muted voice. "Sartish knows where to go."

"How do I know that?"

Sartish's voice floated back to her. "Getting too far behind me, and you just might be taking the quick way down."

"He's right," Azrel advised. "You can't afford not to trust him. Keep moving."

Bella gritted her teeth and strode to catch up with Sartish as quickly as her fear of stumbling would allow.

After some time, Sartish spoke again: "We're here."

Bella looked at the swirling bank of cloud around her, and opened her mouth to ask him where "here" was, when Sartish vanished. She stopped, hesitant, and fear overtook her again. "Go on!"

Azrel's voice commanded, almost in her ear. Bella took a few steps and, as if she had walked through a door, the cloud fell abruptly behind her. She was standing in naked sunlight again.

An expanse of carpet grass spread before her. And here were the children, running back and forth, shrieking with laughter. Farther away stood a bamboo gazebo roofed with coconut thatch, and in the distance, horse-like creatures grazed at the edge of a forest, while leaves swirled above.

The noise of the children focused her attention. They were crowded most thickly at the center of the field. Bella wondered what was going on when a single child rose above the others, bucked around a few times as if riding a very small horse, then rolled off and out of sight.

Sartish glanced back at Azrel. He looked both amused and exasperated.

"At it again," he said.

The children parted before them, staring up at them in wonderment. But even the sight of Azrel failed to distract them for long. They grew more and more reluctant to make way. Sartish had to push the last few children gently aside to reveal what had captivated them so completely.

A young man—he looked about seventeen years old—ran around on his hands and knees, bucking and rolling his eyes in a faithful imitation of a wild horse. At his every movement, the children emitted screams of laughter and occasionally, one tried to get on. He paused just long enough for the child to get settled, then reared up to toss them off, snorting with amusement.

Sartish sighed. "Your Highness."

Bella was incredulous. *This . . . ?*

The young man looked up, shook his head as if whipping around a mane, and bucked around some more. Then he glanced beyond Sartish, noticed Bella, and after circling at a trot, rose to his feet.

"Enough for today!" he cried.

A chorus of disappointment rose up: "More horsey, please, please, please!"

"No," he said firmly. "I have to do some grown-up things now. Off you go!"

More pleas.

"Off you go!" he said sternly.

Slightly subdued, the children trickled away towards the cloud bank. A few resilient stragglers remained, still begging for more horsey, until the young man had to physically shoo them away.

"There's just no pleasing them," he laughed as the last remnant scurried away. He had a round face, dark as coffee, but tinged with cream. He looked as if everything he saw was fascinating.

Either that, Bella thought, *or he's just soft in the head.*

Sartish bowed before the boy. "This is she, Your Highness. I am not absolutely certain she is wanting to be here."

The young man chuckled. "Most people live not wanting to be where they are, Sartish. And her name?"

"As you said, Your Highness."

"Isabella Morgan!" the young man clapped his hands and rushed forward to grab Bella's shoulders. Bella tried to shrug him off, but he gripped her tighter and caught her sullen, elusive eyes with his own. "Tell me, Isabella, do you believe in your dreams when they tell you things?"

"I don't know," Bella said, still trying to evade his gaze, but her heart beating faster at the sound of her full name.

"Well, I do." The young man's grin spread. "And lately, my dreams tell me that you have come to kill me."

CHAPTER FOURTEEN
TEG-TEG SOUP

Bella's heart broke loose, and a cold film spread over her skin. *They know! That damned parrot Crato . . .* It took all her resolve not to break the New Elder's gaze and to keep her expression neutral.

"Believe what you want," she said.

Sartish gaped at the New Elder. "May I inquire as to why you weren't informing us of this, Your Highness?"

Azrel sighed. "You know very well why, Sartish. His Highness wanted the girl to come without interference."

"And why would he be desiring that?" Sartish cried.

"Speak to your Elder directly, Sartish," the New Elder said gently.

Sartish lowered his eyes. "Forgive me, Your Highness. I am simply bamboozled as to why you would willingly let an *assassin*—" he regarded Bella balefully—"within arm's reach of you at all!"

"Why not?" the New Elder replied lightly. "Let her do what she has come to do."

Bella stared at him, nonplussed. *Is he insane?*

Sartish looked equally stunned. "Let her do . . ." he repeated. "Your Highness—"

"I trust that the Wind blows where it wills. Don't you?"

"Of course, but Highness, there's undoubtedly common sense also."

"Ah!" the New Elder waved dismissively. "Overrated, in my opinion."

"So what, then," Sartish said, losing his patience again. "You are wanting me to give her the weapon she brought—" He reached into his pocket and pulled out Bella's switchblade. "You are wishing Azrel and me to leave you two alone so she can cut your throat in peace and quiet?"

"Something like that," the New Elder smiled.

Sartish closed his eyes briefly to get hold of himself. "I cannot be allowing this madness." He looked up at Azrel. "Up to now you won't shut up. Now you're mum. Say something, by the Wind!"

Azrel lifted her hands in resignation. "If His Highness says he is acting in trust of the Wind, what can I say?"

"You can say it is madness!" Sartish shouted.

Azrel shrugged and the New Elder put his hand on Sartish's shoulder.

"Sartish," he said softly. "You must trust me. Give her the knife, and let me talk to her alone."

Sartish said nothing.

"Sartish, please. There is more in this than you and I know."

"I cannot." Sartish shook his head. "I cannot—"

"You can," the New Elder said, and then, with steel in his voice, "and you will."

"It doesn't make sense!"

"It is the way of the Wind," the New Elder said. "And it is my way. Unless you are reconsidering the choices you made . . ."

Sartish clenched his jaw and tossed the knife at Bella. Startled, she caught it.

"You kill him," Sartish told her, "and I kill you. Forget about any reward Hodoul offered. You'll be utterly finished." He glanced up at Azrel. "Let's go," he said bitterly. Turning his back, he strode towards the cliff.

Azrel made a face—part apology, part exasperation—and

muttered a sarcastic, "Yes, sir." Then she said to Jonah, "I will be listening for you. You need only whisper and I will be here." She glanced at Bella before bowing to the New Elder and floating after Sartish.

When they were alone on the plateau, the New Elder turned to Bella and smiled. "Are you hungry, Isabella?"

Bella was too overcome by the turn of events to reply.

"I'll bet you are," the New Elder said. "Come, let's have lunch. Shantila probably put it out already."

He trotted away over the grass towards the gazebo, leaving Bella to follow at her own bewildered pace. When she arrived, he was already seated at a low carved table with a steaming bowl before him. He gestured at a place opposite. "Sit. Shantih-*p'tit!*" He called back over his shoulder. An olive-skinned girl with a round, pleasant face emerged from the trees and skipped over to the gazebo.

"One for Isabella also, please," the New Elder said.

Shantila stared at Bella with frank curiosity before skipping away for another bowl. She placed it in front of Bella, along with a spoon and a napkin, curtsied to the New Elder, and scuttled away.

"She's the best cook I know," the New Elder said, looking after the girl with admiration. "And only six years old!"

Bella looked down at her bowl and recognized *tec-tec* soup.* Disagree had spoon-fed her this while she recovered from the Tree. She felt tears threaten to rise at the memory of his face looking down.

The New Elder raised his bowl into the air. He held it up a moment, then lowered it and gestured to Bella.

"Try it. The best in Mysterion, as far as I know."

Bella's lip curled, but she did not remember the last time she had eaten anything and in spite of herself, went at the soup until every last drop was drained. It was delicious, full of fresh ginger and garlic and made hearty by the rice. Still, it was not as good as the way Dis had made it.

"What do you think?" the New Elder asked eagerly.

"Too much salt," Bella said.

He threw up his hands. "Everyone's a chef!" He went back to his bowl. When he had drained it, he sighed and sat back, staring dreamily out over the cliff at the ocean. The cloud had cleared now, and Bella could once again see the heaving, glittering ocean spread to the horizon.

"I remember when I was a little boy," the New Elder murmured. "We went to the south beach with our buckets. You couldn't swim there because there was no reef and the undertow was dangerous. The waves were huge and green, and they rolled down on the beach, *boom*—like that! And we waited and waited until just as the waves washed out again, then we ran forward quickly quickly to find the *tec-tec*. They're buried usually too deep to find, but when the water runs out they are exposed for a moment. Just for a moment, though, because they start digging right away and if you're not very attentive, they can be gone again, just like that. But if they were just getting under the sand, we always knew where they were . . ."

Because of the mark in the sand. Bella was not sure where the thought came from. She just knew it, that's all.

"Because they left a 'V' in the sand," the New Elder went on softly, marking the air with his finger. "Then we dug as hard as we could and there it was! In the bucket it went *avec son frères** until it was time to go home and boil them up with onions and salt and a little garlic and ginger . . ."

He sighed and was silent.

"I know what you think," he said at last, looking at Bella. "You think I am a slave, and all these people," he gestured at the island below, "all of them are slaves too. You think of Mysterion as a place of liberty, and Monvieil and his people a blot on the landscape, an offense to your freedoms. And the only solution, in your mind, is to conquer or simply eradicate us. That is what they taught you, isn't it? When you came to them from the Nightmare Tree?"

"I don't know," Bella replied in a surly voice.

"Well, I do, because that's what they taught Sartish."

"So you're going to fix my mind like you did with him?"

The New Elder smiled and shook his head. "Not at all. I'm just going to wait. You see, the little memory I recounted was not just nostalgic rambling. There was a point. In my experience, everything is revealed if you just wait long enough. And then, of course, you have to dig . . . But that too will come. Meanwhile, you can stay buried where you are. You may not want to discover the truth, but I promise it will discover *you*, sooner or later. It always does."

Just wait, Bella thought. *I'll show you the truth soon.* "And what's the truth?" she said out loud.

"The truth," he repeated. She waited for an answer, but none came. Then, as she was about to speak again, he said, "Tell me, do you remember your life before the Djinn put you in the Nightmare Tree?"

The question caught her off guard. "That's none of your business," she said.

"You do, don't you?"

"So what if I do? It's none—"

"Didn't you ever find it strange that you alone among the pirates have a memory of your life in Lethes?"

Bella said nothing. When she had come to the Brethren, she had made the mistake of asking a boy named Trent where he had come from before the Tree. The space where one of her molars had been still reminded her of his response. After that, she had quickly learned to say nothing of the memories that swirled just beneath her consciousness, occasionally and briefly surfacing, like the fins of frenzied sharks, before diving again into the murkiness of her daily thoughts.

"You see, I think that's why you are here," the New Elder said, raising one finger. "A true pirate remembers nothing. The Tree empties everyone of their memories, except for you. You remember."

A bruised cloud had rolled up overhead, and now it began to rain—a sudden shower that drew a thundering grey curtain around the gazebo. A minute later, the storm passed. The cloud disentangled itself from the peak and floated on towards the ocean, trailing streamers of rain.

"What's your point?" Bella said sarcastically. "That I'm not one of the Brethren because of a few memories?"

The New Elder smiled and shrugged. "That's the little V-mark. It's up to you to find out what's buried."

"I'm not playing your little head games," Bella snapped. "First you give me a knife and say I can kill you, then you tell me I'm really one of your slaves. Forget it!" She stood and circled the gazebo before turning on him. "I should just cut your throat now and get it over with!"

Infuriatingly, the New Elder laughed and clapped his hands. Bella flicked open her knife and strode forward, pressing it against his throat. "Do that again," she hissed. "And see how funny it is!"

He met her eyes steadily. "Can I show you something first?"

"Why? So you can keep on with your little tricks? No thanks." She pressed the blade harder, and a trickle of blood ran down the New Elder's throat. *Just one slash and it's done*, she thought.

"No tricks," the New Elder said, wincing slightly at the cut. "Just something that belongs to you, that's all."

Bella's eyes narrowed. "What is it?"

The New Elder chuckled. "You will just have to wait and see."

Bella searched his face. She lowered the knife.

"Show me," she said. "And enjoy your last few minutes while you do it."

The New Elder dabbed at the cut on his throat with the sleeve of his shirt and regarded the stain pleasantly before smiling at Bella. "Follow me," he said, and walked out towards the forest. Bella stared after him, then slowly closed and pocketed the knife. She followed him towards the trees.

The horse-shapes Bella had seen earlier now revealed themselves to be a small herd of unicorns feeding on the grass or prancing in circles around one another, bringing their horns together occasionally with a loud *whack!* And what she had imagined were leaves tumbling over the unicorn's heads turned out to be butterflies, diving and swirling in circles. Bella heard shrieks and laughter, and wondered where they came from. Only as the butterflies darted close to her face did she see that they were actually winged children involved in some complicated game of chase and aerobatics with a small white feather that rose and fell in the afternoon breeze. The New Elder stopped to laugh and clap at their antics before leading Bella on.

The undergrowth thinned and gave way. A series of pools lay between the trees, as far as Bella could see. The path split into several branches, but the New Elder did not hesitate. Passing each pool, Bella looked in and below her dim reflection saw a multitude of visions. In one, mermaids herded fish among the wrecks. In another, she recognized the giant seagoing turtle Tala-Qatala, sunning herself on a sandbar. Some sights puzzled her, like one that consisted of nothing more than flickering crystalline shapes. Others seemed familiar in an opaque way—a clock tower, where automobiles circled a roundabout; schoolgirls in striped uniforms skipped along a dusty path; an elderly man sat pensively on the step of his boutique.

"They are Seeing Pools," the New Elder explained, forestalling her question.

"Some of those places don't look like Mysterion." She didn't tell him about her strange new curiosity.

"They see into Lethes—the world we came from—both the past and the future. Ah, here it is."

Bella looked into the pool to which the New Elder pointed. She saw an ancient-looking graveyard lit by the early morning sun, and someone sitting in the shadows, leaning against a headstone. The vision was more than familiar; it stirred something in Bella, a fleeting sense of peace from another time.

"Who is that?" she asked. She felt no real surprise when the New Elder said, "That is Isabella Morgan."

"I liked to sit there," Bella said, before she could censor herself.

"You still do," the New Elder murmured.

Bella frowned. "What?"

"Your entire existence here is just a single moment in Lethes. What you are seeing now is that moment, the moment when you came here, and the moment you will one day return to."

"And this is what you wanted to show me?" Bella said, angry at letting her feelings slip and being exposed.

The New Elder nodded. "I wanted to show you the life you left behind."

"Why? For what reason?"

"So you would know it is there."

"Why would I want that?" Bella cried. "Have you ever considered that maybe I don't want to remember?"

"Because you didn't like it," the New Elder said, "and you ran away."

"Because it was hell! Why would you want me to remember that?"

"Because it's true," the New Elder replied simply. "And because even a real hell is better than a beautiful lie."

Bella drew the switchblade and flicked it open, turning the point on him.

"What do you know about it?" she said in a strained voice.

"More than you think," the New Elder murmured. "Look and see again."

Bella glanced again into the pool and started to see the New Elder picking his way among the graves. He looked more careworn than the person by her side, but he was undoubtedly the same.

"In Lethes, you know me well, Isabella," the New Elder said.

In the pool's reflection, Jonah came up to where she sat against the headstone and squatted down. His lips moved.

Bella looked up at the New Elder. "What is he—you—saying?"

"In his own words, he is saying the same thing I am saying to you now. Come with me, and I will show you a way to a new life. A chance to return to Lethes and find your way back to Mysterion—" the New Elder gestured around— "with your past intact. No escaping and lies this time. Only reality and life as it should be lived. With us, as one of the People of the Wind."

Bella felt a whirlwind of thoughts descending on her. She shook her head. "As one of your slaves, you mean."

The New Elder shrugged. "You would have to submit to the Wind, as it has come to rest in me. You could call that a slavery of sorts, but—" he grinned— "it's better than being a real slave to that Hodoul."

Bella's face drained of its color. She stepped forward, pressing the knife hard against the New Elder's chest.

"I am not a slave," she said.

"Your Highness!"

Bella and the New Elder turned. Azrel was weaving among the trees with Sartish clinging to her back. The Angelus came to an abrupt stop before them, and Sartish leapt off, landing nimbly on the ground between the Pools. He bowed briefly before the New Elder before turning on Bella.

"Was she hurting you, Your Highness?" he said, a little out of breath.

"Of course not!" the New Elder snapped. "I told you I would be fine. And I told you to leave us alone!" It was the first time Bella had seen him angry. The coldness in his voice surprised her.

"Forgive me. It was an urgent matter," Sartish said. "Otherwise Azrel would not be transporting me here."

"Too right," Azrel muttered. "It was an imposition as it was."

"And what was so urgent that you would disregard my express command?" the New Elder demanded.

"The Brethren," Sartish said bitterly, pointing at Bella. "She betrayed us, and the Brethren are attacking."

CHAPTER FIFTEEN
WEST TO EAST

The New Elder, Sartish, and Bella stood at the edge of the plateau. Azrel floated behind them. The sun had descended almost level with their eyes, and the ocean glowed like heated brass. Seemingly embedded on the surface, the approaching armada swelled imperceptibly closer, their sails full in the wind.

"How in the name of everything did they get past the Cyclops?" Sartish said.

"He was probably dead," the New Elder replied, glancing at Bella.

"You mean she killed him?" Sartish cried.

The New Elder considered Bella appraisingly. "I wouldn't be surprised."

Sartish's face turned grey. "He was our only defense," he whispered. "She killed us, too, then." He drew his dagger and advanced on Bella. She whipped out the switchblade and flicked it open.

"No, Sartish." The New Elder moved between them.

"Even after this," Sartish demanded, "you let her live?"

"Yes," the New Elder said, meeting his eyes. "I do."

"It is madness, Your Highness! Like putting your foot in your shoe when you are *knowing* there is a centipede!"

"She's not the centipede, Sartish. You of all people should know that. The centipede, if there is one, is down there." The New Elder pointed down to where the ships had now anchored. The sails were dropping rapidly, and men crowded the railings, readying skiffs to be lowered.

"Hodoul's coming, Sartish," the New Elder said softly. "And I am not wasting any more time trying to stop you from doing what you *know* is not right. Are we speaking the same language, or not?"

Sartish's eyes flickered from the New Elder's face to Bella and back.

"So, you're just going to leave her here?"

The New Elder glanced back at Bella and smiled faintly. "She can stay here if she wants, while we go down and guide the people back. At that time, she will have to decide where she belongs."

"You're not going to fight?" Sartish cried. "The Angeli can bring the swords . . ."

"For the Wind's sake, Sartish." The New Elder rolled his eyes. "Are you going to argue everything I say? There is no purpose to fighting now. Do you not remember the history of Mysterion, what happened the last time we tried to fight those who were inspired by the Djinn?"

"That was different," Sartish said sullenly. "They had the Djinn with them."

"You know very well that the Djinn cannot fight with flesh and blood. No, the People fought their fellow human beings, and they were slaughtered, every one! There's no purpose in it, especially not when it comes to Hodoul. The best we can do now is form an enclave here, and then . . ."

"And then what?" Sartish said. "Wait to die like Tinashe on her hilltop?"

The New Elder looked at him. "You are forgetting yourself."

Sartish lowered his eyes. "But it's suicide."

"I would never abandon the People," the New Elder said. "When they are safe, we will take the next step. I know it is hard for you to understand, but the Wind is in everything that is happening."

Below, the skiffs launched from the ships—oars rose and fell in unison as they darted towards Monvieil's Island.

Sartish watched them for a moment, then said abruptly, "Fine, let's go." He threw a final glare at Bella and began to scramble down the narrow path with dangerous haste, kicking stones off the edge.

"I sometimes wonder if he will ever come around." Azrel shook her head.

"Give him time," the New Elder replied. He turned to Bella. "And what about you? Are you coming with us?"

Bella glanced down to where the skiffs approached and folded her arms. "And why should I help you?"

"Perhaps you shouldn't," the New Elder replied carelessly. "Can I beg a ride down, dear Azrel?"

"You would leave her?" Azrel said, surprised.

"Not you, too!" The New Elder threw up his hands.

"It's not that, Highness," Azrel said. "But supposing she were to try to escape—"

"She won't be going anywhere," he replied, climbing onto the Angelus's back but still regarding Bella. "She wants to belong somewhere, and her only two options are both now present on this island. Think about what I said, Bella," he said, as the Angelus floated off the edge of the plateau. "I will return with my people shortly. You have until then to make a decision."

Bella watched the Angelus descend towards the tree line with the New Elder on her back, her white brilliance answering the gold rays of the late afternoon sun. When they had disappeared into the forest, Bella began pacing around as she chewed the nail of her thumb. Her insides were churning and no matter how hard she tried, she could not bring her thoughts into order.

What will the king do? Would he kill her? Exile her again? The shame of her failure made her shudder. And then there was the New Elder: what she had seen in the Seeing Pool, what he had said . . .

She shook her head and cried fiercely, "Coward!"

Her nervous footsteps turned her back to the edge of the plateau. The sun was now low on the water. The skiffs had disappeared. She guessed they were beaching. From below, she could hear faint shouts, the continuous report of fire rifles, an occasional scream. Then Azrel flashed out of the tree line below, floating upwards. Behind her trailed a ragged line of people—men carrying bundles of personal belongings and women carrying or dragging children behind.

As the head of the crowd wound its way up the slope, the tail emerged from the trees—the elderly mostly, and a few who seemed to be wounded in some way. The New Elder and Sartish followed last, encouraging stragglers who leaned on them occasionally for support on the difficult places. The New Elder carried a child on his shoulders as he strode upward.

Is that all? Bella thought. She had somehow assumed the People would be more numerous than this. But here were no more than two hundred souls at the most, frailer and more pathetic than she had ever imagined. She understood why the New Elder had refused to take up arms. The Brethren, at least ten times their number, would have eradicated them within hours.

An explosion lit up the trees. The crowd stopped to look back and someone screamed. Sartish shouted and drove them forward furiously. As the last of the stragglers started up the narrow path leading to the plateau, the first of the Brethren broke out of the trees, pausing to kneel and fire their rifles. Long flames lit up the sunset-flooded slopes. First one, then two and three people shrieked and collapsed. Azrel turned to gather up the wounded, carrying them up to the plateau in pairs. As she deposited the first inert bodies on the grass, she glanced at Bella briefly.

"Comfortable, are you?"

"What am I supposed to do?" Bella retorted, aware of the horror churning inside her. "Have a good cry?"

Azrel made a disgusted sound and returned for more of the fallen as volleys of rifle-fire broke out below.

The last of the people stumbled onto the plateau and collapsed, panting and weeping, staring around with shell-shocked expressions. Sartish and the New Elder came last, supporting the oldest and weakest on their arms. The New Elder lowered a little girl from his shoulder and pointed her to her family. Then he raised his head and looked over at Bella expressionlessly.

"It's time," he called, gesturing.

With her heart beating painfully, Bella picked her way through the subdued crowd to the New Elder. Sartish watched her come, and she had never seen anyone look at her with so much hatred.

"They have captured or killed more than half of the people," the New Elder said as she came to his side. "This," he gestured at the crowd spread out over the plateau, "is the remnant, and I won't allow any more of them to be harmed. You need to choose now, Isabella, whether you belong with me or with him." He turned and pointed down the slope. The figure of King Hodoul stood less than fifty yards away, and by his shoulder the impassive bulk of Disagree. The sunset lit up the king's angular, crumbled features and glinted in his pile of silver curls as he stared up at Bella and the New Elder, his face utterly still. Behind him and Disagree the Brethren crowded closely, their numbers uncountable down to the trees.

"How are you doing, my dear Bella?" Hodoul called. "Sleeping well at night?"

Shock had turned Bella's skin to ice. She shivered in spite of the heat. Beside Hodoul, Disagree shifted. Bella wanted to run forward to embrace him, but her feet would not allow her to move.

The New Elder was looking past Hodoul now—at Disagree, Bella realized.

"I've seen you before," he said. "You are Isabella's friend."

Bella started. *How does he know?*

Disagree said nothing, but Bella could feel his eyes reaching for her through the dusk. She stepped forward and opened her mouth. At that moment, Azrel appeared beside them, carrying a large, ornate lamp. As Bella wondered if that was really what she thought it might be, the New Elder held the lamp high. The crowd on the plateau fell quiet, except for the whimper of a child and the moans of the wounded. Below, a restlessness swept through the Brethren like a wind.

"Do you see this, Hodoul?" the New Elder said, his voice taking on a new resonance. "Do you know what it did?"

"I have no interest in your little toys," Hodoul's voice rattled up from below. He alone had not been disturbed by the appearance of the lamp. His expression was as placidly indifferent as ever.

"Then why don't you keep coming?" the New Elder challenged.

"With pleasure," the pirate king replied. "Go on," he called over his shoulder.

The Brethren hesitated, milling uncertainly.

"If you value your worthless lives, go ahead!"

"I will go, Your Majesty!" a loud, arrogant voice cried.

Bella recognized the bald head and pigtail of Guillotine, her opponent in the king's challenge, pushing his way forward. He bowed before the king and then looked up and grinned. "No little hussy makes a fool of me and lives to remember it!" He ran at the slope.

As Guillotine approached, the Lamp brightened, as if fueled by the pirate's proximity. Guillotine ignored it, racing forward the last few yards with sweat running in rivulets down his face and bare chest. "Now you get what you deserve, you little traitor!" he shouted, drawing his sword.

A flame flashed from the lamp. It arced outward to incinerate Guillotine before sinking back into a faint glow. Where the pirate had been, a cloud of ash hung in the evening air. Below, Hodoul looked pale. The Brethren moaned and stirred, and some quietly retreated into the night.

The New Elder leaned forward so that his voice would carry down the slope. "The Lamp will protect my People, Hodoul. If you try to come for them, its flame will consume you. You cannot win."

"We won't be leaving!" Hodoul shouted. "And you cannot stay holed up forever, you weak little man!"

"You are right," the New Elder agreed. "So here is my proposal. You do not want my people. You want me."

Hodoul did not reply.

"I will be leaving at moonrise and sailing east, towards the Edge of Mysterion. I will leave the Lamp to protect my people. I will be unarmed. I challenge you to follow me! But only you and your ship. The rest of the armada must release their prisoners and return to the West."

Behind them, the people started spreading this new turn of events.

"You can't, Your Highness," Sartish hissed. "He'll hunt you down."

The New Elder gestured him silent. In the near darkness below, Hodoul's face was a pale sliver.

"Fine," the king's voice rose up. "They will go. And you had better run quickly!"

The New Elder turned to Bella and spoke in a low voice. "Do you remember what I said to you by the Seeing Pools?"

Bella did not reply. She felt as if she were encased in stone.

"Now you must choose," the New Elder said. "Come with me and find out what I meant. Or go back down to him."

"Let her go!" Sartish urged.

"Bella," the New Elder hissed, "decide!"

Bella squatted abruptly and buried her face in her folded arms. Something within her was tearing itself apart.

"I can't," she cried. "I'm a traitor. He'll kill me!"

The New Elder looked down at her. "Then you will come," he said. "And I will give you one last chance."

"One last chance to what?" Sartish cried. "Kill you?"

"Will you keep your voice down?" the New Elder hissed. He leaned over the edge. "And one last thing, Hodoul. I will be taking your little traitor with me. I am sure she will prove helpful to anticipate any little tricks you may be planning. Try to keep that in mind and save your energy!"

"I would be very disappointed in Bella if she did anything like that," Hodoul replied. "*Very* disappointed."

Bella knew the words were meant for her, and she shivered, still crouched down.

"Then you had better get used to being disappointed," the New Elder said.

There was no response from below. Darkness had finally come over.

"I think he is moving," the New Elder said. "Azrel," he called softly. The Angelus, who had dimmed herself almost completely out, fluttered forward. "Go and get Joseph." Azrel floated away and returned a few minutes later. From the corner of her eye, Bella saw an elderly man with charcoal skin and silver hair neatly combed and parted to one side. The old man knelt down.

"Rise, Joseph," the New Elder said. "I have a task for you."

"The rumor is Your Highness is leaving," Joseph quavered.

"I am going east to lead the pirates away from the people."

Joseph made a visible effort to control his distress. "Will Your Highness return?"

"If the Wind blows this way, I will return."

"And the people? They are anxious about Your Highness."

"Take the Lamp." The New Elder handed it to Joseph, who took it with shaking hands. "When the pirates leave, take the people down the mountain and guide them with my authority until I return."

"Your Majesty . . ." Joseph said, holding the Lamp as if it might shatter at any moment. "I am just a fisherman—"

"And I trust you better than anyone. I wish you to do this."

Joseph bowed again. "Very well, Your Majesty. Does Your Majesty wish to address the people now?"

"No. We must not draw attention to ourselves. The pirates will try to trap us before we can sail. Oh, and here is my seal." The New Elder lifted something from around his neck and gave it to Joseph. "In case anyone—Dio, for example," he chuckled, "tries to contest your authority. Now we must go," he said, embracing Joseph. No longer able to hold back his tears, the old man clung for a moment before bowing once more and backing into the night with the Lamp.

"Come, Isabella," the New Elder said, leaning down over where Bella squatted with her head buried in her arms.

"I don't want to!"

"You have no choice now. Either come, or make your way back to Hodoul and face what he has in store."

Bella looked up. "I hate you!"

The New Elder smiled. "Don't shoot the messenger. Now, stand up."

With her jaw clenched in rage and her tangled hair hanging over her face, Bella got to her feet. As the New Elder led the way, she followed with her feet moving automatically. Behind her came Sartish, his eyes burning into her back, while Azrel floated above them, offering barely enough light for them to negotiate the clusters of people scattered over the plateau. They went quickly and quietly, assaulted by an occasional cry as someone recognized the New Elder. But he did not stop, looking neither left nor right until they entered the forest.

Under the trees, herds of unicorns lay together in elegant tangles. In Azrel's light, Bella glimpsed a row of butterfly wings waving serenely in the branches of a jackfruit tree. They threaded their way among the Seeing Pools, sights now invisible in the darkness, until the trees gave way to another plateau. Bella realized that the forest bridged the two sides of the island. The eastern ocean glittered and heaved before them. A full moon was rising on the horizon.

"There she is." The New Elder pointed. Bella lifted her eyes and squinted. Below them on the dark water close in to shore, a sloop tossed against its anchor, as if it would set sail by itself if it could.

The New Elder started forward. Sartish shoved Bella. "Quickly," he snarled.

Bella spun round, her switchblade reflecting moonlight. Sartish's dagger rose instantly and caught her blade with a sharp ring. They stood face to face, pressing and shifting to gain the advantage.

"Enough!" the New Elder yelled.

"Good," Sartish whispered into Bella's face. "That's better!"

"By the Wind, Sartish, stop!"

"Tell her to stop, then!" Sartish shouted back.

"Isabella!"

"Tell him not to push me, or I'll cut out his guts!"

A hand gripped the back of her neck and jerked her backwards, out of Sartish's reach. She saw the New Elder's face, hard under the moon. His hand grabbed her wrist and squeezed until she was forced to drop the switchblade. He left her to massage her wrist and strode over to Sartish.

"Give me the dagger!" he commanded.

"She drew on me!" Sartish protested.

"Give me the knife now, or you can stay here!"

Sartish scowled and looked down at his dagger. Above, Azrel watched in silence. For once, her face was grave.

"Fine," the New Elder said. "You will stay."

"No, here it is," Sartish muttered, holding the blade out. The New Elder took it and in the same motion, tossed it over the edge of the plateau. "Now let's not waste any more time," he said.

"Aren't you going to take hers?" Sartish cried.

"Of course not," the New Elder said, grinning darkly at Bella, who had finally worked some feeling into her hand and was now massaging her bruised neck. "How else is she going to kill me?"

"You're mad," Sartish whispered.

"You just worked that out?" Azrel commented.

The New Elder grinned up at the Angelus. "He's a slow learner. Yes, Sartish my friend, you are certainly right. I am mad by most standards. Nevertheless, there you go. You are stuck with this madman until the Wind changes its direction at least. Now, let's go. Bella, you follow Azrel. Sartish can take up the rear. I'm not letting you near each other for at least an hour."

❄ ❄ ❄

AFTER A TERRIFYING DESCENT down the mountain in which Bella stumbled and fell several times, scraping and bruising her limbs, the ground finally leveled and the vegetation gave way to a narrow stretch of white sand. There was no reef here. Giant waves, black and glistening, rolled unimpeded from the open water to explode on the shore, washing to within feet of the tree line.

Looking left and right, Azrel led them quickly to a small skiff tied above the high tide marker. The New Elder and Sartish launched the boat while Bella watched them sullenly with arms folded.

As the skiff rode the first breaker, the New Elder called to her, "Thanks for the assistance. Why don't you get in?"

Feeling as if someone had wound her up, a force beyond her control now controlling her limbs, Bella waded knee-deep into the foaming water and climbed in. Sartish and the New Elder ran the skiff at the next wave before leaping on board, each manning an oar just in time to take her over the crest and into the deep water. Slowly, they worked their way out towards the sloop, whose movements seemed to grow more eager the closer they approached.

After they had docked, the New Elder turned to Sartish and Bella. "I want to make one thing clear. From this point on, we work together. If Hodoul and his thugs get us, we're all dead—at least while I am still being allowed to live." He winked at Bella conspiratorially.

"So, as much as you two are itching to get your hands on each other, it will just have to wait. All right?"

Sartish scowled. Bella hunched her shoulders.

"Good," the New Elder nodded. "Glad to see you so agreeable. Now let's get ready to weigh anchor."

He looked at Bella. "I assume you are familiar with this?"

"Of course I am!" Bella snapped.

"All right, all right," the New Elder laughed. "Why don't you take foresails. Sartish on mains, and I'll helm."

Half an hour later, the moon reached its zenith in a sky thick with stars. *La Desirée* weighed anchor and slipped out of the lee of Monvieil's Island under full sail. Azrel was a beacon, keeping watch at the masthead. Bella sulked at the bow and Sartish stood grimly at the mainmast, glancing occasionally back to where the New Elder stood at the wheel and searched the horizon as he drove the eager little sloop towards the eastern Edge of Mysterion.

Only minutes after they left, *La Justice* rounded the north headland and set a course in the same direction.

CHAPTER SIXTEEN

THE SHAPE OF MYSTERION

Under full sail, they fled to the east. The empty ocean felt like infinity, and their days acquired a pattern that seemed to have existed for all time. Every morning, they sat on the mid deck, eating fruit and drinking water "from above the heavens" as the ocean turned red and gold and lone clouds scudded across the sunrise. The New Elder spent the rest of the day at the wheel, guiding the sloop with eyes narrowed against the sun. Occasionally Bella would imagine he was asleep, only to see him make a slight adjustment to the helm.

Bella had kept her assignment manning the foresails, but the New Elder had also made her responsible for swabbing the decks, polishing the cleats, and keeping the lines neatly coiled when they were not in use. When she had sulked at the pointless vanity of this task, he had just grinned and winked. "If we're going to be cowards, we might as well be *organized* cowards."

She hated him more than ever when he said things like that.

At the masthead, Azrel spent most of the time glittering in a silence she broke at unexpected moments to drop pieces of sarcasm or irony on their heads. Then, without warning, she would be gone, only to return hours later with a single curt warning: "Two days," or "A day and a half."

"What's she talking about?" Bella asked irritably.

The New Elder looked at her briefly. "Your friends."

Catching a poisonous glance from Sartish, Bella went back to work with the sensation of being torn apart.

Grimly silent, Sartish would man the mainmast until late each morning, when he pulled in the fishing lines he had hung aft and chose a large red snapper or a tuna. He disappeared below to work in the galley, emerging several minutes later with a couple of full pans. He coaxed a wood-burning *marmite** on the mid deck to life, and brought the contents of the pans to a boil. They ate a lunch of brown rice and *bouillon poisson* in the merciless heat of the midday sun, sweating at the chilies Sartish was so fond of adding to his fish stew, trying to put out the fire in their mouths with deep drinks of water "from above the heavens."

Sartish and Bella sweltered away each afternoon in what little shade the sails offered. They moved only to trim the sails, glad for the breeze that washed the deck in a steady stream. As the sun dropped down through the sky, they set to work again—Bella sulking her way through her cleaning tasks and Sartish back down in the galley to prepare their evening meal.

They barely spoke to one another during those days. Bella could feel Sartish's hostility radiating at her whenever she approached, and more than once turned to see him staring at her. She ignored him and went about her duties with renewed intensity, trying to get lost in frenetic activity.

She tried not to think about the reason she was here—the "second chance" the New Elder had spoken of—but it came back to torment her throughout those days. She had not expected his cavalier attitude about his own death, the almost aggressive way he had offered himself to her. Paradoxically, the challenge had proven to be the most difficult of her life—like a wall that rose up insurmountable as long as the New Elder was willing to let her kill him. The situation enraged her, but she found herself helpless to do anything about it.

She spent her sleepless nights on the deck, while Azrel dozed in a dim light or flew away on her reconnaissance missions. These times offered some surcease from her turmoil. The air was cooler and the wind blew steadily at her back while the stars littered the sky and the moon's reflection on the ocean dazzled her with the other side of noon. Sometimes, flying fish rose from the water and rained over *La Desirée* in a gleaming arc. Bella kept a club handy by her side in case one of them misjudged and landed on the deck, flip-flopping. Gutted, scaled, and grilled on the *marmite*, the fish would be a welcome variation to red snapper.

When her thoughts about the New Elder lost their coherence, she thought of Disagree. She wondered how far behind *La Justice* was now, and whether Disagree was standing at the bow railing, wondering where she was. The sight of him standing behind the king in the half-darkness of Monvieil's Island had evoked a pain that had not receded. And if she was to be honest with herself, she wanted nothing more than to sit with Disagree and eat plantains while the birds squabbled in the mango tree beside his shack. To rest in his silence again . . .

"Dis," she whispered to herself, and at once tears welled up within her. Then she clenched her jaw, angry at herself, and returned to the endless circle of schemes to provoke the New Elder into a fight he would not survive, each more improbable, fanciful, and exhaustion-infected than the last.

The New Elder seemed cheerfully oblivious to her struggle. From the helm, he drew their attention to seabirds overhead, or clouds that he compared to this or that person—"Doesn't that one look just like Joseph when he is laughing?" At other times, he commented on the weather ("Looks like a storm heading north. Pity we missed it") or how delicious the food was ("I will never get tired of a good *bouillon*, Sartish!") He never seemed to notice he was speaking in monologue, nor did he seem to see the growing tension between his two companions.

One afternoon, as they sat waiting for the noon heat to give way, Sartish suddenly turned to Bella.

"Do you know why I despise you?" he said.

Here it comes at last, Bella thought.

"Because I am one of the Brethren?" she said.

"No." Sartish shook his head slowly. "I despise you because when I look at you, I am reminded of what I could become in a minute. Do you know—" he leaned forward— "that not a day goes by when I am not being tempted to do what you came to do? Do you not think I am tempted to be slitting his throat?" He gestured with his chin to where the New Elder stood at the helm with his eyes closed. "And then I could be returning to the Brethren, to *him,* and he would have clemency on me and even be rewarding me. Do you think I am not considering this possibility every single day?" His voice was strained, urgent. "And when I regard you, it is by far worse yet. I want it more than ever, I want to do it. I want to kill him just like you . . ."

He broke off and looked away, trembling visibly as he tried to get control. Bella was aware of Azrel's presence above them, and somehow she thought the Angelus was listening intently.

"That is why I despise you," Sartish whispered, barely audible. He stood abruptly and climbed up to check one of the topsails. Bella's eyes followed him, her insides twisted with a strange emotion.

It was as if this encounter had exorcised something in Sartish. In the days that followed, Bella noticed a change in him. Though he was taciturn and distant as ever, his hostility faded to something like indifference. The New Elder must have noticed. After lunch one day, he brought out a chart on a golden cylinder with ornate ends. As he spread the parchment on the deck, Bella drew in her breath.

It was a map of Mysterion, rendered in elegant black ink.

"That's where you both came from," the New Elder said, pointing to the western side of the map and an island where Bella recognized a sketch of Leviathan. "And here is where we are going." The

New Elder moved his finger across the map, past the drawing of Qatala-Tala the tortoise, the mermaids, and Monvieil's Island. "To the edge of Mysterion and the Okean Falls."

Sartish leaned forward. Sensing his interest and a relaxing of the tension between them, Bella wanted to talk.

"I thought Okean was up there." She pointed at the sky.

Azrel answered from the masthead. "It circles Mysterion, like a stream. It rises from the western desert, where the Djinn are exiled, then up and over and down into the east. From there it goes downward into Lethes and up again into Mysterion. A complete circle, though not really."

"What do you mean, not really?"

"It's not really a circle as humans think of it. That's just the way we have to talk about it because you can't understand anything in more than three dimensions." The Angelus shook her head sadly.

"So how does someone get down into Lethes?" Bella asked, feeling the tension return in her again.

The New Elder glanced at Sartish. "You leap off the Edge, and Okean carries you back to the moment you left Lethes. No matter how long you have been in Mysterion, no time at all has passed in your old life. You just continue doing what you were doing at the moment you left."

Bella frowned. "You mean time stops?"

"No." The New Elder shook his head. "Mysterion takes no time at all."

Bella felt a tide of curiosity carrying her. "And what happens when someone comes back from Mysterion?"

"It depends," the New Elder replied quietly.

"On what?"

"On who you are. If you entered Mysterion through the light of the Lamp, Mysterion will always be present with you. However—" he paused. "If you entered through the deceitful magic of the Djinn,

Mysterion will fade swiftly from your memory, like a daydream or a nightmare."

"Through the light of the Lamp," Bella repeated. "Like the lamp you held."

"By that Lamp, yes."

"And how am I supposed to find that lamp in Lethes?"

"You don't need to. I bring the Lamp to you."

Bella remembered the Seeing Pool where she had seen herself and the New Elder talking in the cemetery.

"I still don't understand." Bella shook her head. "How can we be both here and in Lethes at the same time?"

"It's only a seeming contradiction," Azrel said. "All of Mysterion exists in moments of Lethes. If you are one of the People, Mysterion is a moment of truth when you understand who you really are, who you were always meant to be. But if you are a servant of the Djinn, Mysterion is a moment of delusion—a fantasy or a daydream that fades as soon as it passes."

Bella felt her anger and frustration at the New Elder returning.

"So that's why you wanted me to come with you?" she said. "That was the second chance? Believe everything you say, jump off the Edge of Mysterion, and if I survive, forget everything I am here as some kind of lie—all on the off chance that I could learn about your stupid lamp and come back as one of your slaves?" She laughed. "How stupid do you think I am?"

"I don't think you're stupid," the New Elder said, looking hurt and beginning to roll up the map. "And if I thought you would forget everything, I would not have risked everything to bring you with us. This has been done before, believe it or not. Just ask Sartish." He gestured at Sartish, who until now had stared at the map with a dark fascination on his fierce features.

Sartish looked up and nodded. "That was in the time of Monvieil," he mumbled, "when I left Hodoul."

"And here he is now," the New Elder said. "Just as good as new." He smiled.

Sartish did not return the smile. "In Lethes, my papa burned me with cigarettes." Bella glanced at the marks on his forearms. *So that's what they are.* Sartish saw the look and folded his arms. "He was keeping me confined in my room when I was not working. That is where the Djinn was coming to me. He gave me an escape, and I took it." Sartish hesitated. "When they put me in the Tree, I dreamed my papa was burning me until I was black and charred, over and over." He paused. "I found out later that *he*, Hodoul, came for me before the Tree had drained all my memories, because he thought I would be more useful to him that way."

"We think he came for you too, Isabella," the New Elder said. "Did he?"

Bella looked between him and Sartish. "I don't know," she said. But she remembered how Hodoul had come to visit when she came out of the Tree. And then there was what Dis said: *With this or without this, you are a great treasure to him.* Perhaps, she thought, Hodoul pulled her out, too.

"What other explanation is there?" the New Elder said, as if he had overheard her mind. "Go on, Sartish."

Sartish sighed and continued. He told how he had become Hodoul's ward, tending to him all day and night because the king suffered permanent insomnia, until Sartish learned to sleep with his eyes open. He told how he had accompanied the king to parlay with the other crews and forged secret compromises that allowed mutual raids only when it was convenient, constructing fictitious conflicts whose only purpose was to distract the Brethren from their boredom.

He told of the nights in the secret basement of the king's house, when Hodoul needed to make an example of one of the men, not to kill, but to create a lasting impression of what he was willing to do.

Bella shivered at this confirmation of the screams that had floated across the parlay square.

"One night," Sartish was saying, "he decided to use a branding iron to teach someone a lesson. I remembered papa then, how he had burned me all the time. And that was enough. I was done."

"When Sartish came to Monvieil, the Elder who ruled before me," the New Elder explained, "Monvieil sent him back to Lethes. It was a test, I think, to see if he had really succumbed to his old life. But return he did, and in spite of everything, he remains one of the faithful of the People."

Bella, who had been listening with a growing feeling of being trapped in Sartish's story, now laughed unpleasantly. "Oh, really? Then why does he *still* want to kill you for Hodoul's reward, eh?"

Sartish looked at her angrily. The New Elder laughed and gripped his shoulder.

"There is a great difference between wanting and *willing*, Isabella," he said. "Sartish and I have spoken many times about his struggles. He understands the difference, but you have yet to discover it."

He stood and made his way back to the helm. "Let's pay attention. A few changes coming up on the horizon."

CHAPTER SEVENTEEN
THE SOLITARIES

The New Elder was right. All at once, the islands appeared, one after another and sometimes within the span of the same day. Some were deserted—no more than a collection of shrubs and coconut trees fringed with white sand. Others contained lush growths of mango and banana trees, and even a stand of golden-apple trees. In the heart of the forests they discovered hidden streams bubbling from underground reserves of rainwater and refilled their supplies. But signs of human life eluded them until the third evening, when they saw a group of figures seated on the beach around a small fire. They beached the skiff and approached the group, which consisted of several men of varying ages, wearing only loincloths. Further down the sand Bella made out three pirogues, barely visible in the failing light. Bella concluded that these were fishermen, though what they were doing so far out she could not imagine.

"Good evening," the New Elder addressed them. A few younger ones looked up and smiled. The rest did not look up.

"I do not wish to break your vow of silence," the New Elder said. "But I must warn you that the Brethren are pursuing us from the west. If you desire it, you may take refuge on our ship."

There was no answer. The smiling faces returned their attention to the fire, the flames dancing in the onshore wind.

"Listen to the Elder," Sartish said. "You will all be killed!"

"Leave it, Sartish," the New Elder rested a hand on his arm. "They are dedicated to their purpose at all costs."

"What purpose?" Bella asked.

"To keep silence until the Higher Mysterion comes," the New Elder said.

"*When those asleep regain a single tongue,*" Azrel recited, "*which they spoke in the beginning, then we will no longer draw fish from the sea in silent gestures.*"

"Crazy," Sartish said, throwing up his hands. "Everyone here is crazy."

The New Elder smiled and patted his back. "Let's go on. We're losing time."

They sailed on. During the following days, they came upon other groups of silent fishermen, some of them gathered on the beach like those they had first encountered, while others sat in their boats encircling a net. Bella counted thirty-two in the largest group, and the smallest consisted of two old men who fished from a pirogue. They smiled and nodded as *La Desirée* sailed past.

Then an odd exception—a small island where a single woman, partially bald and wearing a tattered shift, had built a hut at the top of a breadfruit tree. As they beached the skiff, she began declaiming something in a garbled language. A host of myna birds, cormorants, pigs, foxes, and moles crowded out of the forest and assembled around the treehouse, listening with complete attention to her speech. When she finished, she reached into a bag and threw them handfuls of food, which the animals ate with enthusiasm before stampeding back into the forest. The woman seemed both blind and deaf to the New Elder's warning about the approaching pirates and the invitation to come with them to the Edge of Mysterion.

"What was she doing?" Bella asked as they weighed anchor again.

"She is also one of the Solitaries," Azrel said. "But she has learned to speak the language of animals." She shook her head. "It always amazes me, the efforts to which some people will go."

The following afternoon, what was to be the last island appeared on the horizon. Unlike the others, the land here was devoid of vegetation and consisted of a series of mushroom-shaped coral formations pushing up against one another. A reef encircled the island, the waves foaming on the white teeth of the coral. Beyond, in the clear water of the back reef, several large shadows moved. Bella supposed they were giant *karung** or dolphins, until a large right-triangular fin cut the surface. It was the first time she had seen sharks. The inner waters were alive with them, playfully charging one another before angling off to circle the island.

"You stay here and keep a watch for Hodoul," the New Elder told Sartish. "I want to show this to Isabella."

"You're going alone?" Sartish said.

"No. Azrel will carry us off."

Carry us, Bella thought. *Why would she carry us?*

Sartish looked at Bella. "But supposing she tries—"

"Then she tries," the New Elder cut in. "And that's all there is to it."

Sartish said nothing more.

As they manned the skiff, the New Elder looked up at Azrel, who was hovering overhead: "Better stay ready."

"Of course," Azrel snorted. "You think *you're* going to get yourselves out?"

"Out of what?" Bella asked. "What is she going to get us out of?"

The New Elder grinned in that infuriating way of his. "You'll see."

They surfed over the reef on one of the breakers. Azrel flew just behind them. The New Elder pulled swiftly for the shore while Bella used a club to beat off the sharks that leaped up to snap at the oars or butt the hull. Then they were aground on the pebbly beach.

They dragged the skiff up until she was firm and had just finished tying her off when a man wearing a loincloth made of seaweed emerged from the dunes and scuttled forward, smiling. He was bald, and his skin had the appearance of being slow-roasted under the sun. His eyes were bemused, as if he were surprised to find himself alive. He ran forward, nodding and gesturing to them to follow.

❋ ❋ ❋

THEIR GUIDE LED THEM through the bulbous formations into the heart of the island. Bella guessed this was an ancient atoll, which explained the lack of vegetation, but she could not imagine who could survive here.

"Where is he leading us?" she asked the New Elder.

"To the Keepers of the Phoenix."

"Who?"

"You'll see," the New Elder repeated.

"No need to treat me like a child!" she snapped.

Abruptly the hills fell behind them, opening onto a patch of blinding white sand. Men and women, all of them hairless and burned and wearing the same makeshift seaweed clothing, lined the edges of the clearing. At the center lay a circular pile of twigs several feet in diameter held together with seaweed. An arched wall decorated with a large mural partially enclosed the pile. As they came closer, Bella saw that the mural was an intricate mosaic made of colored shells depicting a young woman at the peak of a cloud-wreathed mountain, her hands upraised. Dark, winged figures descended on her.

Their guide waved them forward again before himself disappearing into the crowd. Everyone seemed to be waiting for something, their eyes fixed on the pile of twigs. They opened a way before the New Elder and Bella without turning to look at them. Bella would have pushed her way in to get a closer look, but the New Elder touched her arm. "Not too close."

She spun around. "I am sick and tired of your—" she began, and then stopped. The New Elder was staring back towards the center of the clearing. Bella followed his gaze. An elderly man had stepped out from the crowd and was facing the wall and the untidy pile of twigs. He raised his hands to the level of his waist, palms upward, and began to chant something in a low singsong voice. Bella could not understand the language, which consisted of clicks and moans and low hums. Then she became aware that Azrel was hovering beside her shoulder.

"What language is that?" Bella asked.

"It is our language," Azrel whispered, as the old man began to shuffle back and forth. "The language of the Angeli. He is one of the People privileged enough to speak it, though his accent is atrocious."

"We know," the New Elder murmured. "No one's good enough to talk like you. Just tell us what he's saying."

"He is telling of the beginning, how the world was made as one whole, and how all things spoke one language."

Bella could tell that Azrel was summarizing the old man's words as he shuffled in slow circles, alternating back and forth, with his hands still raised and his eyes closed in a kind of ecstasy.

"But the Djinn tempted some away with dreams of another life, and the People were divided. Brother fought brother for many generations. Angeli fought Djinn by air, man fought man by sea . . ."

A brief memory jumped into Bella's mind—water running over her skin, wrecked ships looming suddenly out of the green water, then vanishing behind as the mermaids sped her on to the east.

That was the great battle, she thought.

"And the People fell, until only one remained. Tinashe was a girl and no warrior, but steadfast and brave, and the Wind guided her diamond sword against her foes, until she too was cut down."

A clicking sound could now be heard over the old man's

chanting, which had stepped up in pitch. He was no longer moving, but stood swaying as he faced the pile of twigs. The clicking was coming from inside the pile, a sound like sticks being tapped together, heavier sticks.

"The Djinn swarmed over Mysterion for a hundred years. Their human allies, the rebel Letheis, lost themselves forever in sleep and dreaming. And their dreams gathered generation by generation, like streams running into a single ocean. So came into being the world of Lethes."

The skull of a giant bird rose over the edge of the pile of twigs, which Bella now realized was an enormous nest. It peered around sightlessly at the crowd and swung towards the elder's chant. Its fan-like wing bones beat awkwardly in the nest as it balanced on its skeletal claws and ruffled nonexistent feathers.

The bird skeleton emitted a wheezy shriek. The old man did not miss a beat of his chant. His voice rose another pitch. Glancing sideways, not wanting the New Elder to think she was nervous, Bella saw his eyes were fixed on the skeleton. Azrel too was staring at the skeleton, watchful now, as if she were waiting for something. Still, she continued to translate the song.

"As the Letheis were entombed in their dreams, Tinashe lay where she fell, forgotten. Her body went the way of the earth, but it was not lost, for on that fertile spot Monvieil grew up like a vine."

Skin was growing over the bird skeleton, while inside it, organs bloomed and swelled with miraculous speed. Moments later, the bird's innards disappeared from view, concealed by a brand new pink layer of flesh. Feathers swiftly sprouted until the bird stood fully enlivened, decked out in magnificent gold and green plumage waving like delicate fingers.

The old man's voice rose to a falsetto. He was shuffling in circles again, and the crowd now had broken its stillness, swaying side to side. Azrel continued: "In the fullness of time, Monvieil fell upon the occupying Djinn and burned them up with Wind-fire and cast them back into chaos. And then he slept and dreamed his way into Lethes, waking the Letheis to Mysterion again."

The bird now reached the peak of its radiance. Spreading wings, it emitted a piercing shriek. All the light of the late morning broke from its feathers, glinted off a scimitar-shaped beak wrought, it seemed, of pure gold. Bella was forced to narrow her eyes and lift her hand to fend off the brilliance. She found herself holding her breath, caught up in an unexpected awe at the sight. Even as she did so, however, she sensed the light's intensity dimming. The bird's feathers now seemed duller than the moment before, still glossy but fading quickly.

"But even as the People returned to Mysterion, the Djinn returned to tempt them, to undo the work of Monvieil. They fed the human race to their Tree and its black fruit. And those whom the Tree at last sucked dry they left abandoned among the Brethren to live out their deaths forever."

The bird's feathers had turned the color of ashes. A few wisps of smoke drifted off its body.

"Almost time to go," the New Elder muttered.

Azrel seemed to ignore him as the old man continued. "Then came Jonah in search of his father," she translated. "And he entered the Tree and destroyed it with his love, and once again the Djinn were cast into chaos. And this one Jonah, Monvieil made a new Elder among the People—"

"Azrel," the New Elder repeated more urgently. Smoke enveloped the bird. The crowd around them swayed in unison, their heads bowed in expectation. Only the old man stood still, addressing the bird with his song.

Bella realized what was about to happen. She understood why none of the people around them had any hair and wondered how they had survived so often. She looked at Azrel. But the Angelus's eyes were fixed on the bird—intent, serene.

"And in time he will lead us into the Higher Mysterion, where death and rebirth will be no more, and you, O Phoenix, will shine brighter and brighter, that all may see you without blindness!"

At last, the old man fell silent and bowed his head with the rest of the crowd. The phoenix exploded into flame. Azrel grabbed Bella and the New Elder and rose so quickly that Bella felt as if her stomach had been left behind on the ground. The phoenix's flame swelled outward, licking tongues at Bella's heels as Azrel continued to soar skyward. Bella's ears popped as they gained altitude. Then the flame slowed and mushroomed out over the island—a single great cloud of smoke rolling in on itself across the water.

"Cut it a bit fine, didn't you?" the New Elder's voice was breathless.

"We couldn't leave before the end of the song," Azrel explained. "It would be inappropriate."

From the cloud below Bella could hear the faint sound of chanting.

"They're alive," she said, somehow not surprised.

"That's their life." Azrel shrugged, floating over the cloud towards where *La Desirée* was anchored. "They sing the song of our history and endure the phoenix's flame. Until the Higher Mysterion."

"What are they saying?"

Azrel gave her a strange look. *"Break into wholeness, empty into fullness, surrendered to victory."*

CHAPTER EIGHTEEN
RAISING THE EDGE

B ella woke to the sound of Azrel shouting on deck: "They're on us! They're on us!" The New Elder called something in reply. Against the hull the water had taken on a different sound: urgent, almost frantic. Bella could tell from the angle of the hull that they were reaching under full sail. *La Desirée* hummed like the low string on a violin as the wind pushed her on.

She slipped out of bed and pulled on her clothes. Pushing her tangled hair behind her ears, she ran out of the cabin and up on deck. The New Elder was already at the helm. He greeted her with a grin.

"They made it at last," he said, gesturing aft with his chin.

In plain view, no more than fifty leagues aft, *La Justice* bore down upon them, every sail on her yards bulging.

Sartish's voice, strained and angry, descended from above: "I still don't understand how they surprised us!" He was working in the rigging of the mainsail, swinging around from line to line.

"They didn't," Azrel replied from her perch at the masthead. "I've known they were coming for several days."

"Then why didn't you say something?" Sartish shouted.

Azrel shrugged in the New Elder's direction.

"Because they need to know where we're going," the New Elder said.

"You wanted him to find us." Sartish stated the fact.

"Of course," the New Elder replied. "How else would Bella be able to get back to her friends?"

"So what now?" Sartish asked, glancing at Bella. "We just die? For her?"

The New Elder rocked his head. "Not quite yet. You seem to have forgotten that we've reached the Edge."

Bella swung around. High above, stream-like currents streaked the surface of the sky, flowing downward. Lower, the air shivered and then ran down like wet paint, smearing and swirling to the line where the horizon should be. Where it collided with the ocean, a white wall rose up, a cloud of mist rolling and boiling, breaking sunlight into multiple rainbows.

A faint, continuous roar drifted towards them in the wind—immense, but distant.

"But it is too late," Sartish cried. "They will catch us before we are even reaching the line of mist!"

The New Elder smiled. "Only if they can follow us through the shallows."

Sartish hesitated. He looked beyond the bows. Several leagues distant, the green of the ocean broke out into blue patches. In places, white foam marked the teeth of a reef beneath the surface.

Sartish turned back to the New Elder with narrowed eyes. "You know the way through, Your Highness?"

"With my eyes closed," the New Elder said. Then, unaccountably, he laughed.

Sartish looked back at the approaching pirate ship. It was close enough now that the name was clearly visible on the bow. The crew crowded the railing, some of them waving swords and fire-rifles.

"Will we be reaching the shallows, though?" Sartish wondered.

"We won't if we keep talking," the New Elder replied. "There's a topsail luffing and we need every knot."

Sartish looked up to where the fore gaff fluttered above, spilling wind. All argument vanished. He snapped to life and shinnied upwards. A moment later, the fore gaff filled again. Sartish moved among the rigging, adjusting the lines before slipping down to the deck. "We need the spinnaker up, Your Highness," he said, glancing at Bella. "A reach won't do the trick."

"Good thinking." The New Elder nodded and spun the wheel counterclockwise. Immediately, *La Desirée* turned off her broad reach. Her aft came up as the wind roared full at her stern. Behind them, *La Justice* matched her move precisely. Bella wondered if Ah-Time was at the helm, or perhaps Disagree . . . Horror filled her. She was running from Disagree. And yet she was running from Hodoul also. Perhaps there was still a chance to show *him*, and all this could end.

At the bow, Sartish had opened a small hatch and was dragging the bulk of the spinnaker out onto the deck. Wrestling and slipping for several seconds in the mass of silk, he finally managed to get the hook on the lines. Then he was hauling up the sail, which fluttered and twisted in the force of the wind. Around him the sheets tangled, impeding his progress.

"Want to help?" the New Elder asked Bella with a smile.

"Why should I?"

"No reason." The New Elder shrugged. "Just wondered if you wanted to see Hodoul before I'm dead."

Bella looked at him, then back at *La Justice*, now almost within a fire-rifle's shot of the New Elder. If the spinnaker didn't get up soon, it would be minutes before they were boarded.

And then she would stand before *him* again.

Just a little more time, she thought. She turned and strode aft to where Sartish still struggled with the sail.

He glanced up at her. "I'm fine," he said, and went back to wrestling with the slippery material.

"I'm sure you are," Bella replied. "And you'll be even finer hanging from the main yard of *La Justice*."

"You better go away," he hissed. "Now."

"You don't want my help?" Bella asked. "Fine, then." She turned away.

"Sartish!" The New Elder's voice came clearly and deliberately from the helm.

Sartish looked back. On *La Justice*, the crew lined the railing. Snipers waited in the yards for firing range.

Sartish shifted his eyes from the oncoming ship to the New Elder, then to Bella.

"Find the foot of the spinnaker," he muttered. "I will keep working on the head."

Bella went to work. Together, they unwound the tangle of silk and rope. With Sartish guiding the head, the massive, balloon-like sail rose, spread, and bulged over the water. *La Desirée* leapt forward. Waves crashed down on them in regular, drenching succession.

Having closed the gap even further in the minutes they had lost raising the spinnaker, *La Justice* now seemed to be holding its distance. But even as Bella watched, the frigate adjusted its course to fall directly aft of *La Desirée*. Above, the spinnaker sagged, collapsed, then refilled before collapsing again. The other sails were doing the same now—catching the wind, then flapping uncertainly. Bella glanced at Sartish, and then back at the New Elder. From their aghast expressions, she knew both of them had realized that *La Justice* had stolen their wind.

"Shallows ahead!" Azrel shouted from the masthead.

Sartish spun around. The patches of dark and light blue and the reefs were less than a league distant. Beyond them, the wall of mist and the thunder of Okean's stream falling towards the Edge.

"It's too late!" Sartish shouted back at the New Elder. "They will be upon us before we are getting there!"

The New Elder said nothing. He closed his eyes and continued to steer them towards the shallows as quickly as the fickle sails would allow.

Yards behind them now, *La Justice* was preparing to board. At the railing, men crowded with coils of rope and grappling hooks. And there, standing among them at the bows, familiar and incongruous as a mountain, was Disagree, staring across the water at them with a look that paralyzed Bella even as it knocked her heart loose.

"Trim! Trim!" Sartish shouted at her as the spinnaker fluttered and collapsed. Bella did not even turn around. Sartish exclaimed in exasperation and grabbed the line from her, pulling it in until the sail filled again. *Justice* was angling off slightly now to overtake them. But even as she did, the wind, no longer obstructed by her bulk, now fell with full force on *La Desirée*, and the sloop leapt forward. All her sails snapped tight. White water exploded on her bow.

For an instant, *La Justice*'s bow was level with their stern. Then, incrementally, she began to fall back. Several men raised their fire-rifles, and for the first time, Bella wondered that they had not done so before now. Then, over the wind, she heard a faint shout. She tore her eyes from Disagree and looked aft. King Hodoul stood by Ah-Time, the helmsman. The king's bush of white hair tossed around, and his crumbling features stood out even from a distance. He leaned forward with a kind of intentness, as if driving the ship onwards by the force of his will, and slashed the air with his hand. He shouted again—a stentorian order.

He doesn't want them to fire, Bella thought. It didn't make sense, unless . . .

Hodoul was calling something forward again. Disagree turned his head, listening for a second before hefting the grappling hook above his head. The men around him retreated as the hook swung in a wide circle. Disagree released, and the hook arced high overhead, hit *La Desirée*'s aft deck with a crack and caught in the railing. Bella felt a check in the sloop's movement.

"Sartish!" the New Elder shouted. "I can't let go of the helm!"

Sartish was already running aft, and Bella saw he had a hatchet in his hand. Seeing him go, she felt a kind of desperation sweep over her. Dis had thrown that line to her, and now Sartish was going to cut it.

Dis, she thought.

The paralysis that had overcome her dropped away, and she began to run after Sartish. Leaping over cleats and ropes with an agility she had almost forgotten after long weeks on board ship, she reached him just as he raised the hatchet over his head, about to bring it down.

"Bella!" the New Elder called. Bella ignored him, grappling Sartish around the neck and pulling him backwards onto the deck. They wrestled fiercely for precious seconds as *La Desirée* bucked against her leash and *La Justice* began to close in. The crew now stood on the railing, ready to leap.

"Reef on the starboard bow!" Azrel shouted above. At the helm, the New Elder closed his eyes and took a deep breath. He held it for a long moment, frowning slightly, as if trying to see something inside his head. Then, suddenly, he opened his eyes and spun the wheel. *La Desirée* turned, and a booming to starboard announced they had just avoided the reef.

Sartish pinned Bella down at last. With his forearm on her throat, he groped around for the hatchet, found it, then leaped up and as Bella grabbed out for him, dove at the rail, slashing downward.

The rope parted with a crack. *La Justice* fell back and groaned as it rose up on the submerged reef. Men tumbled off the railing and fell screaming into the foaming green water. At the helm, Ah-Time spun the wheel frantically. The sails collapsed. Rigging twisted and snapped.

Only Disagree in the bow and Hodoul in the stern remained untouched by the chaos that descended on the ship, now dead in the water. Bella could feel both their eyes across the widening gap— Hodoul like a hand gripping at her, trying to hold her. Disagree's hand was a different sort—held out in a gesture that broke her at last.

She was curled up in fetal position and sobbing uncontrollably as Sartish stood over her, his face stony.

"Now do you see?" he asked the New Elder.

"No," the New Elder said. His eyes were still closed as he navigated the shoals and hidden reefs. The wall of mist loomed higher. Behind, the pirate ship was now anchored and riding easy.

"You saw what she tried to do," Sartish said softly.

The New Elder opened his eyes and regarded Sartish. "Would you have done differently, Sartish Kutty?"

Sartish's mouth worked slightly, trying to form an answer and finding none.

"You cannot dispense with your past so easily as that," the New Elder said.

Sartish's face turned grey. He stared at the New Elder's serene face, then down at Bella, who was still weeping. Abruptly, he choked out a groan and stumbled away to disappear below decks.

"If you would be so good as to lower the sails, Isabella," the New Elder said. "We have almost arrived."

Bella sobbed.

"Don't worry," he murmured. "You will have one more opportunity to do what you came to do. However, if we do not get those sails down, we will all be going over the Edge, like it or not."

Still weeping, Bella raised her head. The mist-bank was closer than she had expected, as if they were moving faster than their sails could drive them. She heard a rushing sound around them, an urgency in the current. She scrambled to her feet and looked over the rail. The water around the submerged barriers had turned to rapids, carrying them forward in a rush towards the Edge.

Bella went into action. Several minutes later, only the topsails remained. "Keep those up," the New Elder said, as she made to lower them. "We will need some maneuverability."

Barely ten yards ahead, the mist bank swirled in and out on itself, as if something were boiling deep within it. As Bella fought to catch her breath from the furor of lowering the sails, the ship swept into the bank. The reefs and shoals and the anchored pirate ship vanished behind a curtain of mist. The current ran in a solid grey-green rush. The thunder of falling Okean blocked all incidental sounds.

"We are here," the Elder said.

As he spoke, a great twisted shape, like a mutated hand, loomed suddenly out of the mist bank. Bella recognized it at once, and the shock of seeing it here, so far from *that place*, drained the strength of her legs. She hugged the mast and clung on to stop herself from collapsing on the deck.

"After the unmarked island was destroyed, this thing was all that remained." The New Elder shouted to make himself heard. "A charred remnant of the Djinn. It is here as a warning of what could be again."

The great shape solidified now, blackened from the fire that had consumed it two years after Bella had emerged from its hollow center, the dark womb where her nightmares were born and reborn—a great, twisted baobab tree that seemed to be floating on the surface of the rapids.

Azrel spoke. "In the Higher Mysterion, it shall stand as a record of the New Elder's first conquest."

"We must tie up on it," the New Elder said.

"No!" Bella cried.

"There's no other anchor between here and the Edge," the New Elder said. "Take the helm—quickly!"

Bella pushed herself away from the mast and stumbled over to the wheel, her legs buckling beneath her. The New Elder, after making sure she had a firm grasp on the spokes, ran lightly to the bow and prepared a grappling hook on a line. "Bear starboard!" he yelled over the sound of Okean. Bella obeyed mechanically. As they slipped past the great twisted baobab, the New Elder whirled and tossed the hook. It landed among the branches and caught fast.

Quickly, the New Elder tied off the line on two large cleats. *La*

Desirée came up short against her new mooring. The branches of the Nightmare Tree creaked, but held. The topsails fluttered as the schooner turned up into the wind, tracing a wide pendulum path in the current. Then she came to rest, her bow pointed against the current that drove on past towards the Edge of Mysterion.

CHAPTER NINETEEN
THE NEW ELDER'S DREAM

Bella moved down the passageway leading aft to the master's quarters. Around her the sloop creaked and rocked against the current. The water hurried past the hull in a steady gurgle and hiss, so Bella did not attempt to conceal the sounds she might make as she went. The switchblade hidden in her fist was cold and heavy and somehow alien. She gripped it harder. At Sartish's cabin, she paused and bent her head. He might be waiting behind the door for the telltale sound of her step. She allowed a full minute to go by before going on. Reaching the master's cabin door, she eased the latch open and slipped in, closing the door quietly behind her.

The master's bed lay directly before her. A faint light descending from the portholes along the upper walls outlined the rest of the cabin: a small bureau of drawers built into the wall, narrow benches on either side of the bed, a tiny door she supposed led to a miniscule bathroom.

The New Elder lay on his back, covered only with a sheet. From the way his hands were folded on his chest and the expression of humorous indifference on his lips, Bella imagined he was already dead. Then a faint snore emerged from his lips.

Her hands drenched in cold sweat, even in the stifling heat, she opened the switchblade and stepped up to the bed.

He opened his eyes and regarded her calmly. "I had that dream about you again."

"I don't care," Bella said.

"You never asked what I dreamed. Why is that?"

"Are you deaf? I'm not interested in your stupid dream."

"Then grant me a dead man's wish," he said with a playful smile, "and let me tell you what it was."

"If you think more talk is going to change my mind . . ." Bella pressed the point of the blade against the New Elder's bare chest. He winced slightly at the prick, but made no move to avoid the contact. A solid black spot emerged in the gloom where the tip broke his dusky skin.

"No," he said with a tinge of breathlessness. "I just thought you might want to know why I allowed this."

Bella held the point in place, gathering herself to drive the blade into his heart.

"Why would I care?" she said.

"Because my willingness was an obstacle to you. Probably the most implacable enemy you have faced. Only the sight of your friend this afternoon, the desire to return to him, overcame it at last."

Bella stared at him. "How do you . . ." She shook her head fiercely. "Never mind! You have one minute to explain."

"I dreamed you were running in the darkness," the New Elder said. "There were trees around, branches whipping at you, but I couldn't see them. I was looking down on you, as if I was flying above. And that man, the big one who stood behind Hodoul, your friend . . ."

Bella shook slightly, pressing the point harder, turning the black spot on the New Elder's chest into a little rivulet that trickled down his side and onto the mattress. The New Elder winced and went on. "He was running beside you, but you could not see him because he was away to one side, parallel and hidden by the trees. There was a light ahead, a house. Your friend angled away, and I could see him going on up the hill towards a hidden place where he could rest. But you ran on to the house and climbed through one of the windows.

"In the next moment—you know how dreams are—I was looking down inside the room, and you were curled on a bare mattress like an unborn infant. I could hear people shouting nearby, a man and a woman—your parents—and you were holding your head and trying to shut out their noise. But you couldn't do it, and you began to rock from side to side more and more violently. Then you looked up and screamed that it was my fault, it was all my fault." He stopped speaking and smiled at her. "And that was the dream. That was how I knew you would be coming to kill me, and that was how I knew your friend."

Bella was pale, her knife arm extended stiffly, as if it had been frozen there.

"I know who you want to be, Isabella Morgan." The New Elder spoke very softly. "And I know who you *are*."

Tears spilled out of her eyes. Her mouth opened, but several more seconds passed before words emerged: "I can't."

"Then don't."

"No," Bella said. She flung the switchblade onto the carpet. She went to the door and looked back, her face twisted. "I don't deserve to live. I failed and I'm going back to face it, that's all!"

The New Elder said nothing. She turned her back on him. Throwing open the door, she raced down the passageway, not caring if Sartish heard her, and then up the steps onto the deck, where a wind of mist-fine rain swept over her, cool after the oppressive heat below. She looked up to the masthead. Azrel had not returned. Bella felt a trace of relief that she would not have to endure the Angelus's sarcasm. However, even the thought of it brought the hot and bitter bile of shame in her throat, and she hurried aft.

Hand over hand, she hauled the skiff in against the current. It came reluctantly, and she wondered if she could pull hard enough to make any progress against the current. But it was too late to hesitate now.

She climbed into the skiff, set the oars, and released the line. Immediately, the current pulled her aft the sloop. She pulled hard and her regress slowed. Stationary for a moment, she slowly regained the distance she had lost, until the skiff came level with *La Desirée* again. Bella dipped and hauled, her body aching and drenched with sweat and mist. After long minutes of effort, the sloop fell gradually aft. The mist curtains drifted across, concealing the ship from view.

At last, Bella became aware that the current was easing as she put more distance between the skiff and the edge of Mysterion. The skiff's movements took on a less strained quality, the bow cutting more and more easily through the short waves. The mist bank, too, receded, and white stars pricked out above her. The moon broke out above, spreading a sheet of light on the ocean. Mere feet behind her, the wall of mist rose up, lit up and swirling against the moonlight.

She was clear. Fighting to catch her breath and calm the wild beating of her heart, Bella rested on the oars and looked around. Almost at once, she spotted *La Justice* drifting a hundred yards ahead. There was something both ghostly and predatory about her, like a memory of a hundred raids coalesced into a single ship. Bella shivered. She knew they would spot her before she reached them, but she was surprised at how close she came before a low voice called out:

"Identify yourself!"

"It's Couteau," she replied as clearly and steadily as she could manage. "Bella Couteau. I request parlay!"

There was a brief silence. A rope ladder dropped over the side, unrolling as it went. Bella grabbed a rung and clambered upwards. On the deck, shadowy figures immediately surrounded her.

"I want parlay," she repeated.

From directly ahead of her, a deep familiar voice rumbled: "I never believe I hear that from you, little Bella."

Bella began to tremble. "Dis?"

Disagree moved forward, a mountain of a shadow. "That's my name."

Bella ran forward and threw herself into her friend's arms. Her sobs came in great heaves and gulps, as if she had surfaced from a great depth. Disagree held her as if he had been carved there for all time.

Someone said, "Your little friend come home, eh?" A round of snickers echoed around them. Bella detached herself.

"He's expecting me, isn't he?" she asked Disagree.

"Of course," Disagree replied. "He knows you come." She could not tell his expression in the darkness.

"Then take me to him."

As Disagree led the way, the crew parted reluctantly. They descended the steps. The passageway was unlit except for a thin strip under the master's cabin door, which only exacerbated the darkness until it crushed Bella's heart. The snakes had come alive in her stomach again.

Disagree knocked at the Master's cabin door. At the muffled assent, he pushed it open, standing aside. His face was impassive as ever, but she noticed the strained lines of exhaustion around his eyes. Reaching out to touch Dis's arm as she passed, Bella stepped through the doorway.

King Hodoul sat in the center of the cabin, wearing a simple linen nightshirt. His disordered curls glinted in the light of oil lamps. Before him a table was laid with platters of fruit, steaming crabs in their shells, and a roasted red snapper garnished with breadfruit fritters. A loaf of bread lay at his elbow, along with a flagon of palm wine and two brimming goblets.

His face reminded her of an eroded gravestone as he picked up one of the cups and raised it to her in greeting.

"I waited to have dinner," he said. "Now that you are here, we can eat."

CHAPTER TWENTY

OF HERMIT CRABS
AND ROBBER CRABS

King Hodoul gestured Bella to a stool beside his carved chair and said, "Thank you, Disagree. I will call when we need you."

"I want him to stay," Bella said quickly.

A corner of Hodoul's mouth twitched. "You and I have some important matters to discuss, young lady. Things may be said that may make it difficult for you to remain friends with Disagree."

"I don't care. I want him to stay."

"I go," Disagree muttered.

Bella's eyes pleaded with him. "Please, Dis."

Disagree hesitated, then glanced at the pirate king. Hodoul shrugged. "Stay then. Just keep your mouth shut."

"He can say whatever he wants," Bella said.

"He can keep his mouth shut!" Hodoul slammed his hand down on the table, his face white with rage. "Or he *will* leave, and you will get what you deserve! Do you understand me?"

Bella stared at him, her jaw clenched and her heart racing.

"Sit down," Hodoul told her. He ignored Disagree, who closed the door and stood immobile in the corner.

"Have some crab," Hodoul said, suddenly solicitous.

Bella hesitated, and the king's mouth twitched again. He placed two steaming crabs on her plate and then served her fish and fritters. Then he gestured for her to eat before tucking into his own plate. Bella began reluctantly, but soon got lost in the rich and spicy flavors in which she could detect Disagree's hand. He had overseen the great feasts the king had thrown following successful raids. Great trestle tables piled like this, encircling a great bonfire around which drunken Brethren leapt and whirled in absolute abandon with their female partners, sometimes falling into the flames to be dragged out again, singed and smoking, shrieking with laughter and pain. She tasted something both sweet and bitter in those memories now, as if she had lost them forever.

Across the room, Disagree seemed to mirror her mixed enjoyment of the food. At one moment, he regarded her with what she thought was pleasure. Then the lamp flickered and he seemed sad, almost pitying. The light shifted again, and he was inscrutable as always. Bella shook her head.

Hodoul too was looking at her now, smiling. "You can taste it again, eh? I told him you would. Didn't I, Dis?"

Disagree nodded slightly. "I do it—she remember."

"That crab was just perfect, too," Hodoul kissed his bunched fingers. "If you boil them too long in the coconut milk, they get soggy. But not this, not this . . ." Then he fell silent, admiring the food.

"Remarkable creatures, robber crabs," he murmured. "Not only delicious when cooked in milk and spices, but admirable characters as a whole. I saw one climb a tree once, pick a nut, climb down, and open it within a minute. Another time, I saw a fellow chasing one because it had stolen a piece of his wife's jewelry. He cornered the creature, used a club to try to get the jewelry, but you think that crab lost out? It turned and chased the fellow right back to his house with the bracelet or whatever it was held tight as ever in its claw." Hodoul chuckled hoarsely and rocked back in his chair, looking at Bella through lowered eyelids.

"Enterprising creatures," he continued. "*Strong* creatures, you know? But the really interesting thing is—" he raised one finger— "and I want you to listen carefully, my dear Bella, the interesting thing is that the robber crab does not start off strong. Do you know how they start off life, hmm?"

Disagree shifted slightly in the corner, and Bella glanced at him before answering the king, "No, I don't know."

"They start as *hermit* crabs. You know those?"

An image flashed into Bella's mind: a hermit struggling on its back just before she brought her foot down on it. She had not realized how strongly that insignificant act of cruelty had stuck with her.

"Despicable creatures," Hodoul was saying. "Scurrying from shell to shell, fighting over the skeletons of the dead." He shook his head. "A waste of the Wind's creative energy, if you ask me. And for its infancy, at least," he emphasized these words, "the robber crab resembles one of these hermits. It too is small and uses a borrowed shell to protect itself from predators. But the key difference is that unlike hermit crabs, which aren't real crabs at all, by the way . . ."

Bella looked towards Disagree, thinking, *What is he going on about?*

"Forgive me." Hodoul's voice drew her eyes back. "I do love a good analogy. Almost done, if you will indulge me."

Bella shrugged. "I have time." She did not understand where this new confidence was coming from.

"Not quite as much as you think," Hodoul murmured. "But we will come to that. Now, what was I saying?"

"Hermit crabs are not real crabs," Bella muttered. She picked up a breadfruit fritter and took a nibble.

Hodoul nodded. "That's right. Hermit crabs never acquire a shell of their own. They're always scurrying from one borrowed home to another. And if they can't find a bigger shell, they don't grow any bigger. And then they can be eaten, much as I eat these crabs right now." He paused with a grin, and suddenly Bella became aware of a meaning beneath his words, like the shadow of a shark beneath the water, and the nervous tension from before flooded back into her.

"But the robber crab is different. When it is old enough and strong enough, it emerges from its shell. And then it is free to do whatever it pleases and no one can touch it." Then he broke off with a laugh and picked up a claw. "Well, almost no one, anyway. *Everyone* has a natural predator."

He cracked open the claw with his teeth before sucking out the flesh. He dropped the shell into a bowl now overflowing with broken remains and wiped his mouth, his eyes never leaving Bella's face.

"Do you see my point?" he said.

"No," Bella replied, though she definitely felt uneasy now.

Hodoul leaned forward. "Well, let me give you a hint. What is that you are wearing around your neck?"

Bella looked at him, caught off guard. "What do you mean?"

"Don't play with me!" Hodoul snapped. "Around your neck! What is it?"

Bella touched the place where her medallion hung. "It's mine."

"Show it to me."

Bella hesitated, staring at him defiantly.

"Show it to me!"

Bella pulled out the medallion on its cord. It hung against her shirt, glowing warmly in the lamp light.

"What is it?" Hodoul asked.

Bella hunched her shoulders sullenly. "A doubloon. It's mine, I didn't steal it!"

"I didn't say you did. But do you remember where you got it?"

Bella was chewing on her fingernail now. "My father gave it to me. Before . . ."

"Before you came to Mysterion."

"Yes."

"It was one of his few gifts to you, wasn't it?" He was leaning close now, eyes glittering in the broken face.

Bella felt a dizziness come over her as she stared at the pirate king. "How did you know that?" she whispered.

"I can tell you more than that. I can tell you that it belonged to one of your ancestors, a pirate. That it was passed from generation to generation. That it was a constant reminder to your family of their origins, a point of pride that came from bold adventurers, plunderers, *robbers.*"

Hodoul's face filled Bella's vision, blocking out the rest of the room. Somewhere nearby she could feel Disagree, somehow locked out now behind the overwhelming presence of the pirate king. Somewhere inside her she could hear her father's voice, very far away: *Remember where you came from, ma fille. It wasn't always we were like this, living in crap. We were strong.*

"Do you know the name of the pirate to whom that doubloon once belonged?" Hodoul asked, almost gently.

Bella shook her head, but she did. It all made sense now. Hodoul nodded, having seen the answer in her eyes.

"Only one other person knows the story of how I came to Mysterion," he said, glancing at Disagree. "It happened on the day I was hanged for piracy. They brought me out to the main square. There was a good crowd that day, the best they ever had, I was told." A bitterness tinged his smile. "They read the verdict: piracy, rapine, murder, and so on and so forth. Then they asked if I had anything to say. I asked them to free my hands. At first they wouldn't do it, but I convinced them in the end. So I stood there looking down at those landlubbers. Then I took that coin—" he pointed directly at the medallion— "and held it up in the air so they could all see it. Then I said, 'Find my treasure, whoever is able!' and I threw it into the crowd."

The silence that filled the cabin pressed down on Bella like a solid thing. She was utterly paralyzed by it.

"I didn't just throw that coin at random, though," Hodoul continued softly. "I wasn't going to let just *anyone* have it. I threw it to my beloved Natalie, who had stood by me in all the years of my wanderings. She didn't hide herself away that day, either. She stood right at the front, and hers was the only face free from disgust in that crowd. She alone showed some pride at that moment, and I saw her catch that doubloon and hide it in her bodice before anyone knew what was happening. She was always good at making gold disappear." He chuckled.

"In the uproar, they led me to the gallows. That was where the Djinn came to me, disguised as the hangman. How could I resist? He held out the pendant, and I took it just before they pulled the lever."

Hodoul's words sank into silence. His face seemed to recede, and Bella could see Disagree in the corner again.

"You probably know that those who return to Lethes return to the moment they left," Hodoul said. He did not wait for her response. "If I ever go back to Lethes, I will go back to the moment I died. Which is why I can do things that living people would never dare to do. Do you understand?"

Bella tried to nod, but she still could not move.

"But of course, everyone wants continuation, progeny. Even people like myself. Which is why, when the Djinn summoned me about two years ago and informed me that they had imprisoned someone wearing that medallion around her neck, I was more than interested. We made a little trade, they and I. They got something I had been willing to give up a long time ago."

"What was it?" Bella asked in spite of herself.

"What was it?" he echoed, staring at Bella.

"That is not your concern!" he snapped. "All you need to know is, in exchange, I got you before the Nightmare Tree had completely drained you. I got you with some remnants of your memory intact, so you could be useful still, not just one of those—" he gestured at the deck above them— "those dregs. You could still remember a little of your life in Lethes, enough, anyway, to know how you got that medallion and perhaps even how important it was." He paused a moment to let the words sink in. "And when the time was right, I could find a reasonable, a legal way to bequeath my achievement in Mysterion to you. The assassination of the New Elder provided just such an opportunity. When I learned you had stolen Granbousse's Claw powder, I thought I had found just the thing to motivate you: a choice between exile and death on one hand—" he lifted his left hand— "or an act of daring and inconceivable reward on the other." He demonstrated with his right hand. Then he looked between them. "I thought it would be sufficient to put a little steel in your back when you weakened, but . . ." He allowed the rest of the sentence to drift away, his eyes now baleful and cold.

"Which brings me to my little excursus about crabs," he continued. "You see, my dear Bella, I think I understand why you hesitated to do what you knew you had to do with the New Elder. When you joined them, they convinced you that you're really one of them—a little hermit crab. And because you are young and impressionable and perhaps you feel as if you are weak inside, you started to think the shell you had crawled into was really your own. But it wasn't, you see." Hodoul's voice rose to a shout. "Because you are *not* a hermit crab! You are a robber crab, and you have been *since the very beginning*! Am I making myself clear?"

Bella's head jerked. Hodoul's eyes now gripped her face.

"You cannot escape the past, my little robber crab. And that is why you will go back now and complete your task. You *will* do it and you *will* receive the gift I am offering you! Or else I may have to conclude that you are not who I thought you were, that you really are a hermit crab. And in that case, I will have no trouble in eating you alive and consigning myself to damnation."

Hodoul sat back and drank deeply from his goblet. He was breathing hard and his face was flushed.

"I have nothing more to say to you," he said at last. He told Disagree, "Take her back to her boat and let her go."

Disagree spoke for the first time, and Bella heard the strain in his voice: "Your Majesty, I say something."

"I don't want to hear it. Just do as you are told!"

Disagree met Hodoul's implacable stare for an instant before lowering his head and leading Bella into the dimly lit hallway. They climbed back on deck, where the crewmen were huddled in groups. They crowded forward now, firing questions at Disagree from every direction.

"What he say?"

"She'll be hanged, no doubt?"

"Or keel-hauled, right?"

Disagree silenced them with a sweeping gesture.

"The girl has business for His Highness that's none of your business."

"Come on, Disagree. Give us a word!"

But Disagree had turned to stone again, pushing forward so they had no choice but to give way before him while they muttered about favoritism, and who the hell gave him the right to keep things from them, and if it weren't for the Code, they would tickle him into talking with a dagger. When they reached the ladder, Disagree turned to Bella for the first time. She was aware of the men pushing closely from every side. Their stink was overwhelming.

"When you finish your job," he said softly, "you light a beacon at the masthead. I come to get you then."

"Bring a skiff," Bella replied, shivering slightly. "The current's too strong."

"You letting her go?" someone cried.

"He's letting a traitor go!"

Disagree's head found the source of the voice. "Shut up, Cauchemar."

"Or what?" Cauchemar replied.

"Come here and you see," Disagree replied.

Cauchemar pushed his way forward, a square-shaped man with a scar that left his mouth in a permanent grin.

He leered up at Disagree. "What now, Monsieur Disagree?"

Without warning and without any effort at all, Disagree grabbed Cauchemar by the throat and lifted him into the air. He swung him over the side and let go. With barely enough time to scream and clutch at Dis's hand, Cauchemar fell and hit the water with a loud explosion. He sank at once and a second later resurfaced, screaming and flailing and slapping at the surface.

"He can't swim!" someone shouted.

"Then you best get him," Disagree said. "And let me follow my orders."

Calmly, he turned away as the crewmen scrambled to man ropes and rescue the hapless Cauchemar.

"Go now," he said to Bella.

"Come with me," she said. Her voice was quivering.

"No," Disagree said. "He don't let me."

"Why?" Bella cried.

"Because I am a slave," Dis said heavily. "Even here, I am always a slave." He regarded her. "Just like you."

Suddenly, Bella knew it was true. She was precious to Hodoul, all right—just as all possessions are precious.

All this was a lie, she thought. The flame that had been guttering inside her went out. Disagree reached out and lifted her over the rail. Her feet found the rungs of the ladder, and she reached out to steady herself with one hand, while clinging to Disagree's arm for a moment with the other.

"Please, Dis," she begged. "Please come."

Firmly, with a strength far beyond hers, Disagree pulled her hand off his arm and planted it on the ladder.

"Too late for me," he said.

The men had succeeded in hoisting Cauchemar over the side, and now he lay coughing and heaving on the deck.

"You almost killed the bugger, Disagree," someone commented.

"Not that he didn't deserve it, mind you."

"When we get back," Cauchemar rasped between coughs, "you can start digging your own grave, *Kaf.**"

"Go now," Disagree growled at Bella. "They start up again." He turned to Cauchemar's sodden form. "So you want some more lessons. Let's go then." Cauchemar wailed involuntarily and the men drew back. Feeling as if her flesh were tearing with each movement, Bella climbed down the ladder and leapt into the skiff. Fumbling with the ropes, she finally untied the bow-line and the boat drifted away from *La Justice*. She manned the oars and began to pull, though she had no idea where she was going or how she was going to find *La Desirée* again. Still, her arms kept pulling, and though it felt as if she were rowing through tar, *La Justice* soon fell behind. The first fingers of mist drifted past. A white hand closed around the boat, blotting out the panorama to aft. The moon vanished, the stars overhead were blotted out.

Bella became aware of something behind her. She looked over her shoulder. Azrel's familiar light floated in the mist. It was dim, barely more than a brighter patch of mist, but unmistakable.

Confusion assailed her. Had they known she was coming? But why would they guide her back, unless . . . She could not find the reasons, but somehow she knew this was her last hope of refuge.

The current now carried the skiff forward. Bella used the oars to keep the skiff pointed at Azrel's beacon. As she approached, Azrel's light dimmed. The Angelus was taking no chances, keeping her light as faint as possible on the off-chance the pirates caught a glimpse of their location.

La Desirée loomed suddenly out of the darkness. Bella angled off, pulled in the oars and reached out just in time to grab the rope ladder hanging amidships. She shinnied up the ladder. Once over the railing, she secured the line on a cleat and paused a moment to catch her breath.

She looked up at Azrel. "Thank you."

"Not my choice," the Angelus replied, and dimmed herself almost to extinction.

He told her to guide me back, Bella thought. She felt her heartbeats speed up. Something thrashed inside her.

A dark shape, more solid than the New Elder's, appeared from below decks.

"Coming to finish it off?" Sartish's voice shook with emotion.

Bella was suddenly shaking. "I want to see the New Elder."

"You will have to be killing me first!" Sartish replied.

Until that moment, Bella had not known what she was going to do.

"You don't understand," she said, stepping into an abyss. "I want to stay."

CHAPTER TWENTY-ONE
A TIME TO DISAGREE

Bella stood at the railing, looking down at the New Elder and Sartish in the skiff. Azrel fluttered around, agitated.

"Is this wise, Your Highness?" the Angelus said for the third time.

"There's no other way, Azrel," the New Elder replied patiently. He smiled up at Bella. "This is why we are here."

"I know," Azrel said, "but—"

"I am still not believing it," Sartish declared. "What's the game?" he asked Bella. "What did he hatch this time, eh?"

Bella was shaking and no words would come out. She just shook her head.

"That's enough, Sartish!" the New Elder snapped.

Sartish hunched his shoulders, glanced at the New Elder and muttered something. The New Elder ignored him, looking up at Bella with an expression Bella did not recognize.

"What will you do?" he asked, though she had explained everything beforehand.

Bella shrugged, feeling tears welling up within her again.

"Are you sure?"

"Even hell is better than this," Bella said quietly.

The New Elder took a deep breath and nodded.

"I will see you," he said softly.

Bella folded her arms. "Whatever you say. Now go before I change my mind!"

The New Elder raised his hand, but Sartish did not look at her. The skiff pulled slowly away. As they disappeared, the New Elder's voice floated across the water. "Remember the Keepers of the Phoenix."

Bella said nothing, nor did she raise her hand in response. She felt as if every living being had deserted the universe and every source of light had been put out. Several minutes passed before she became aware of a presence above. Azrel sat at the masthead, looking down at her inscrutably.

"What do you want?" Bella asked.

"I'm staying here," Azrel replied.

"I don't understand."

Azrel looked at her for a long moment before responding. "Do you know what an Angelus is?" she said finally.

Bella shook her head.

"We are witnesses," Azrel said. "From the beginning of the People, we have watched and listened and borne witness to your life. At times we conversed with humanity and even got involved, but that is not our first task. Our first task is to see everything, to witness to everything. We gather events, moments of sadness and horror, laughter, silliness . . ." The Angelus's voice drifted away.

"I have seen infants being born and infants dying, old people dying and old people being born also." She laughed. "I get sarcastic because that's who I am. Every Angelus has a way of letting off steam. Some say nothing, some just weep, others get angry or laugh all the time. Me, I can't help but see the irony in everything. I have to roll my eyes because if I didn't, I couldn't stand it anymore. I'd have to run away above the heavens."

"So that's why you're here," Bella interjected. "To *spy* on me?"

Azrel chuckled. "We always see," she said, "so what you do may be known."

"Who cares about what I do anyway?"

"Everything matters," Azrel replied. "Everything must be gathered in so that the story may be told in the Higher Mysterion. That is what we have been given to do—we gather so the Wind can tell."

"Whatever you say," Bella said. "Just don't watch me, that's all!"

Azrel tilted her head. "What are you afraid of?"

"I am not afraid. I'm . . ."

Azrel tilted her head. "What?"

The word came painfully: "Ashamed."

"Ashamed of what?"

"Betrayal. Failure. I was weak . . ." Suddenly tears were running down her cheeks.

"Weakness is not such a bad thing," Azrel said.

"Yes," Bella shouted back. "Yes, it is!"

"So why did you come back? Why let them go?"

Bella just shook her head. Azrel sighed and looked off into the distance. The thunder from the Edge of Mysterion filled the silence. Azrel looked down again.

"So you really want me to leave you," the Angelus said.

Bella nodded, thinking, *No, please stay . . .*

Azrel inclined her head. "Then I will go. But I will still watch from above."

"Why can't you just go away?"

"I told you," Azrel said calmly, "everything must be seen. You have always been seen, from the beginning. For example—" a mischievous smile crossed her lips— "you were seen—not by me, someone else—when you stole Dragon's Claw powder from Joe Granbousse and then smoked it."

Bella felt her face growing hot.

"You want to be alone," Azrel continued. "You always have. But no one is alone, Isabella. At least not now."

"If you have to watch, then watch," Bella said. "Just don't let me see you. I can't stand your face any more!"

Azrel shook her head and clicked her tongue. "That would really hurt, if my face were not just something I put on to give you humans something to look at. Oh well, I know when I'm not wanted." She floated upward without perceivable effort. "Goodbye Isabella," she called down softly. "And may you find some use for your weakness after all. Such a waste, otherwise. Either way, I will be watching." She faded into the streams of mist and darkness.

Bella sat down and hugged her knees as a hurricane of emotion gave vent to its fury. She gripped tighter as if trying to crush herself, and when this did not succeed, she stood up and paced the deck. At last, she stopped in front of the mast and looked up. She knew there was a lamp up there. It had remained unlit at night while they had Azrel, but now it awaited a single lit match.

"Light a beacon," Dis had said. "I come for you."

Bella fumbled around in her pockets, but found them empty. She ran below, fumbling in pitch-dark cabins until she located a box of matches in a galley cupboard. She found something else too—a small hatchet—before climbing back up on deck. She ran to the bow and hid the hatchet within easy reach.

Amidships again, she clambered up the mast until she was swaying back and forth, while mist-laden gusts swept over her. After several attempts, she kindled the lamp, and a sphere of light pushed back the darkness. She might not have believed anyone existed beyond that sphere, but exist they did, and she knew it would not be long now before they came for her.

And then . . . she thought. A fit of shivering overcame her, so violent she almost lost her balance. Her skin was cold now, and not just from the mist. She climbed down to the deck and made her way to the bow. The branches of the Nightmare Tree clawed at the darkness above her. The rope that anchored *La Desirée* to the Tree was taut as a metal bar, the only thing preventing her from being swept towards and over the Edge of Mysterion. Bella leaned back against it, staring out to the edge of the lamplight where they would be coming from.

The splash of an oar came to her over the distant thunder and the sounds of the wind and current. It was close, but Bella found it difficult to tell how close. She stood still. Every nerve ending in her body seemed to have acquired the gift of sight and now stared into the mist.

A skiff broke out of the darkness, shadowy in the lamplight, driving down the current past *La Desirée*. Bella recognized the massive figure at the oars at once—Disagree. Joy flooded through her, only to be twisted into terror as she saw another figure in the aft, hunched and unmistakable.

Disagree worked the oars to bring the skiff around against the current, then pulled her back until she came amidships with *La Desirée*. With a crab-like movement, Hodoul slipped forward and grabbed the rope ladder. Leaving Disagree to secure the skiff, he hauled himself up and onto the deck. A moment later, Disgree pulled himself over the edge and took his customary place behind Hodoul, facing Bella. She waited for them in the bow, now utterly still.

"Where are they?" Hodoul said quietly.

"They're gone," Bella replied, her voice trembling. "I let them go."

The pirate king chuckled—it was not a pleasant sound. "You dared to defy me," he said. Drawing his rapier, he stepped forward. Disagree reached out and grabbed his shoulder, preventing him. Hodoul whipped around. As his dagger swept backward, Bella grabbed the hatchet at her feet and raised it high over the rope that anchored *La Desirée* to the Nightmare Tree.

"Don't!" she shouted. Hodoul paused and turned. Slowly, he turned back to her, sheathing the rapier.

He chuckled again, this time with genuine mirth. "You must be joking, Bella Couteau. You would dare to send us all over the edge? You would go back to being a pathetic creature in Lethes? I appreciate a heroic gesture as much as the next man, but this is just silly.

Besides, you'd need to cut more than once to get through that rope, and by then we'd be on you. So why don't you put down your little piece of foolishness and let's try to talk maturely, all right?"

Bella did not move, but the hatchet swayed in the air. Hodoul saw the movement and nodded. "You see? I can be reasonable, too. Do you think I would kill my own flesh and blood? Really, now."

"You'd kill anyone who crossed you!"

Hodoul shook his head sadly. "My only descendant? My posterity in this life? You must think I have no humanity left. No, I would never do that. A little punishment perhaps. What is life without consequences, after all? But death is out of the question. I swear it on Leviathan."

"You expect me to believe that I would come back and not be in your debt for the rest of my life?" Hodoul said nothing, staring at her implacably, and Bella went on. "Since when were you giving away forgiveness? I know better than that. I know what your 'mercy' costs!"

"I don't know what you mean," Hodoul said softly.

"Tell him, Dis," Bella said. Her arm was starting to hurt, so she lowered the hatchet, resting it on the railing. Hodoul's eyes followed the movement all the way down, but he did not make a move.

"Tell him," Bella repeated. Disagree said nothing. "Fine, then I will." She addressed Hodoul, surprised at a sudden calm that had descended on her. "When Dis came to the Brethren, long before me, he was alone. No one would call a small fat black boy 'brother,' so they chased him and beat him, but you did nothing about it. Then one day, some other boys tried to hang him. They almost did it, but you happened on them and they ran away. You brought him down, and when he was better you told him you rescued him, but you never punished the ones who tried to kill him. Not even a lashing. You disobeyed your own law . . ."

"How dare you hold *my* law over my head!" Hodoul shouted.

"And you indebted him to you. He believed he owed you his life!"

"He did. I rescued him!"

"You think he's a fool?" Bella retorted. "He found out what really happened, but he stayed with you. You know why?"

"I think you had better stop talking," Hodoul hissed.

"Because he believes everyone needs someone who loves them. Even you!"

The pirate king's tone was mocking. "Oh, that's so touching, I think I might just have a good cry. Isn't it touching, Dis?" He looked at Disagree, who moved his head in a way that Hodoul took for assent. He swung back to Bella. "You see? You think Disagree is a child like you? He made his choice to stay loyal, and he has reaped the reward. Far more than if I had just left him hanging." He snickered slightly at the joke. "So what if I showed a little mercy to those scamps? That is my right as king of the Brethren. I won't be lectured by some immature little turd who thinks she can stand up to me just because I told her we're related! Don't presume on me, Bella Couteau. My patience has almost run out. Drop that hatchet and come back with us. I can still prevent you from suffering the full consequences of your gross error, but only if you do exactly as I say—right now. This is your last chance—wisdom or folly!"

Bella looked at him, then slowly raised the hatchet upward again. As it hung in the silence, Bella spoke:

"Send Disagree to take it from me or it comes down."

Hodoul did not hesitate. "Take it, Dis," he snapped. "Let's be done with this!"

Disagree took a step forward.

"Faster, man. Do it!"

Disagree continued on at his chosen pace, slowly approaching Bella at the bow. Three feet away from her, he stopped. Bella could feel his eyes pressing into hers—an almost unbearable weight.

"Take it!" Hodoul spoke each word distinctly.

"Yes," Bella said. "Take it, Dis. Take it all away from me."

Disagree took another two steps forward, reached out, and grabbed Bella's hand with his own, engulfing it. And that's where he stayed, holding up the hatchet with her, looking into her eyes.

"What are you doing?" Hodoul screamed.

Bella felt Disagree's hand, heavy around hers, pressing down. Her heart broke loose. She stared at him.

"You sentimental fool!" From the corner of her eye, Bella saw Hodoul start forward, drawing his sword.

"He's coming," she whispered to Disagree.

"Then cut it," he replied softly.

Her arm shivered, muscles aching under the almost dead weight of Dis's hand.

"I'm scared," she whimpered.

"Yes," he said. "But you be all right if you are."

"I'll teach you!" Hodoul shouted, striding forward, turning his blade flat to whip Disagree across the back.

"Now!" Disagree commanded, his voice louder than she had ever heard it.

For an instant, the New Elder's last words came to her: *Remember the Keepers of the Phoenix.*

Break into wholeness, empty into fullness, surrender to victory. And for the first time, she understood.

"I hope so," Bella whispered. She closed and allowed her arm to collapse under the full weight of Disagree's arm, bringing the hatchet down. The blade sliced cleanly through the rope anchoring *La Desirée* to the Nightmare Tree. The rope parted with a loud *crack!* and the sloop was free, slipping rapidly backward in the current towards the Edge of Mysterion.

CHAPTER TWENTY-TWO

GUTTING LOOSE

Hodoul froze, his arm in the very act of delivering the stroke to Disagree's back.

Disagree turned to him. "You get back in the skiff. Now."

La Desirée was swinging around in the current, the deck heeling as she drifted sideways, swifter now.

"You killed us," Hodoul whispered.

"Yes," Disagree agreed. "If you don't get into the skiff."

Even as his face crumbled with fear, the pirate king turned on Bella. "I should kill you where you stand!"

"Then you kill me too," Dis replied, "and you row that skiff yourself. *If* you can."

"You're going back with him?" Bella cried, grabbing his arm. "Dis . . ."

"Go," Dis told Hodoul, who stood panting with rage, his sword shaking. "I come behind you right now."

Bella shook Disagree's arm. "You're coming with me!"

"I won't let her back," Hodoul snarled. "Not even if she begs!"

"She do not want to," Dis said, ignoring Bella's pleading expression.

The roar of the Edge was louder now, though still out of sight. The mist too was thicker, more like an opaque wall of water. Any moment they would come to it. Nausea coated the back of her throat.

"Get in now," Disagree said to Hodoul.

The pirate king hesitated. "Are you coming?" he demanded.

Disagree nodded, and Bella felt herself grow cold.

"You'd better!" Hodoul snapped. "I can't believe you'd join her in this foolishness!" He turned on his heel and strode aft, holding onto the railing to balance against the wild movements of the ship. As he reached the ladder, he spun around. His face was pale in the tossing light of the masthead lamp.

He reached his hand out towards Bella. "Last chance, Couteau!" he shouted. "There's no mercy after this. You'll forget everything. You'll die an insignificant layabout on the street with two or three snotty brats hanging off you. I'm offering you one last chance. Against my better judgment, one more chance at greatness."

"Shut up!" Bella screamed. "Shut up!" She looked up at Disagree. "Please, Dis."

"No," Dis said sternly. "You make this choice. You do not make it for me."

"But you're going back with him?"

Bella thought a smile crossed Disagree's face. "As you say," he said, "everyone need someone who love him."

She could find no reply for that.

"Disagree!" There was a definite note of fear in Hodoul's voice now.

"I come!" Disagree shouted. He placed his hand on Bella's shoulder. She threw her arms around him and clung until he gently disengaged her and lumbered back amidships to where Hodoul waited at the ladder. Seeing him come, the pirate king threw Bella one last poisonous look before disappearing over the railing. Disagree untied the bow-line, leaving a single loop to hold the skiff to *La Desirée*. Bella ran towards him. Hodoul had settled himself in the stern. Disagree pulled the boat close. The skiff rocked and tossed as he leapt on board.

"Careful, damn you!" Hodoul shouted in panic, perching on the transom. Now at last he was a pathetic figure, terrified and utterly dependent for his survival on Disagree, who ignored him as he set the oars to the oarlocks. When he was ready, he looked up at Bella, pale at the railing.

"When you come back I see you again," he said.

"Come back?" Hodoul cried. "She's not coming back!"

"You keep quiet!" Disagree roared suddenly. "Or we all go over!"

Hodoul was sullen, cowering in the stern.

Disagree looked up at Bella again. "You find me," he said.

Bella shook her head. "Dis."

"What?"

Then tears were streaming down her cheeks. "I love you."

Disagree nodded. "I love you also." He tossed the rope away from him. As it slipped up and around the railing, Bella caught and held onto it. The weight of the skiff dragged her forward.

"Let go," Disagree called.

Bella clung on—then with a shudder, dropped the line. Disagree wound it up, manned the oars, and hauled to work the skiff around against the current. For several seconds it seemed as if they would make no progress. Disagree heaved with all his strength. The skiff fell slowly behind.

La Desirée was now drifting broadside to the current. The sound of the Edge beat on Bella's eardrums. The water was dark and unblemished, with only the occasional flash of foam to indicate its speed.

The mist parted. Okean was a wall of water streaked with the light of the stars and the moon, stretching infinitely upward and to either side. At the level of the horizon, the foam was a solid barrier.

Looking aft, Bella saw the skiff at the edge of the mist-line and Hodoul gesticulating wildly. Disagree pulled, obviously exerting all of his immense strength, and after hovering in view, the skiff made incremental headway against the current and vanished back into the mist.

Feeling as if she had finally been separated from her body, Bella turned to face Okean. She ran aft and grabbed the aimlessly spinning wheel. Straining, she worked *La Desirée* around until the sloop pointed at the Edge. No longer resisting the current, the ship slipped into Okean.

"I want to remember!" she shouted, but her voice was lost in the thunder. And then she was into the white explosion. Solid water thundered down over her, the ship breaking up before everything dropped away beneath her. Silence descended suddenly as she floated past the Edge. And then she was alone in an endless waterfall of gold light, breathing an air far lighter than air.

LETHES III

Jonah Comfait sat on the rocks looking out over the ocean. The sun, newly risen, shattered on the surface. The monsoon breeze exhaled endlessly in his face. Jonah closed his eyes and took a deep breath before glancing at where the takamaka tree stood, like something ready to collapse.

I should do this, he thought. *It's getting late.*

The sense of futility overtook him again. After all, it wasn't as if he hadn't tried to help her. Perhaps it had been premature, but her reaction still scalded him—that vindictive, jeering expression, as if she had almost been looking forward to saying what she had said: "A magic lamp? Grow up!"

How long are you going to push this? he asked himself. Another part of him responded, *For as long as it takes!*

Jonah jumped to his feet and clambered up to the takamaka tree. He rolled away the small boulder that covered the opening and reached in, then snatched his hand back as something scuttled over it. A hermit crab wearing a tiny conch shell ran out and disappeared into a crevice in the rocks below. Jonah reached in again and pulled the Lamp from its hiding place. With both hands he carried it to a flat spot and set it down.

He had seen it countless times, but every time he looked, it exerted a new hold on him, as if it had recreated itself yet again. Nothing physical had changed, of course. It was still the same three-foot-high, minaret-shaped lamp that Captain Acquille, his old mentor, had presented to him—was it only two years ago now? The polished surface threw sunlight back in his face, forcing him to narrow his eyes to see the ornate grillwork pattern around the Lamp's core: fishermen on an ocean full of fish, Angeli fluttering above on their bodies of multiple wings.

As familiar as always, yet holding another depth he had never seen. What was it? He had struggled with the question of how ordinary things could get deeper. Then he recalled how Captain Acquille had struggled to learn the Lamp, and with what result? Nothing, until a dream had come to him and revealed the hidden meanings he had sought with such futility. In the end, Jonah thought, perhaps he could never know the Lamp completely until it *wanted* to be known.

A movement at the corner of his eyes distracted him from his speculations. His mother was making her way among the rocks, leaping up onto a perch when a wave ran in before coming on towards him. She wore a blue floral dress today and had plaited her hair into intricate pigtails that wound around the back of her head. As Jonah watched her, all the disappointment and futility of the past two years reached a high point. If only she, at least . . .

He shoved the thought aside—he had been over it too many times—and forced himself to smile up at her.

"I thought I'd find you here," she said.

His mother sat beside him, tucking her skirt between her legs.

"Madame Morgan telephoned," she said.

"Oh?" he said. "Now what?"

"Isabella ran away again last night. Madame Morgan said she stabbed her father almost to death."

Jonah exhaled slowly. He felt his shoulders sinking under an invisible weight.

"She was exaggerating, of course," his mother said, chuckling. "It was really no more than a deep scratch. He's just fine. I could hear him in the background, whining and complaining like a child."

"It's not the first time either," Jonah muttered. "He should be used to it by now."

"Is this worth continuing, you think?" his mother said. "Isabella doesn't seem to be making any progress, and I am sure Monsieur Gontier wasn't expecting you to stick this long with the tutoring. If she doesn't graduate, she doesn't graduate. You can't achieve the impossible."

"I need to go," Jonah said. "She talks to me."

"She could talk to someone else," his mother pointed out.

"No, she can't."

"Why?"

Jonah was silent.

"Does your going there have something to do with this?" His mother gestured with her chin at the Angeli's Lamp.

Jonah shifted uncomfortably. "If it does?"

"You want her to believe?"

Jonah looked at her defiantly. "Why not?" It sounded ridiculous, even to him.

His mother looked at him steadily. "You know you can't make it happen."

"I thought you of all people would understand," Jonah said suddenly. "You believed when I told you!"

His mother held his eyes for a moment, then sighed and turned to look at the sea.

"Yes," she said. "I believed what happened to you and your father, even when he denied it." A smile briefly crossed her lips. "I believed it like I believed the dreams that told me you would both come home safely. But, Jonah—" She turned to him, her eyes begging. "As time went on, I realized there are other things more—" she struggled to find the words— "more, I don't know—"

"More important," Jonah said bitterly.

"No." She held up her forefinger. "Not that. Just things that needed to be secured in the meantime, if you know what I mean.

Your father wanted to rebuild his business, and I had to work hard to make sure he didn't take us down the same path as before. That's why I'm doing the books now. And all of that was just more urgent than Mysterion, as wonderful as it is—" She broke off, seeing his expression, and sighed again. "I knew you wouldn't understand."

"I understand," Jonah said. "You're doing what Papa did. We weren't back five minutes when he wanted to pretend that nothing ever happened. No Djinn, no tree, no Monvieil. A stupid shipwreck!"

His mother looked at him. "That's not true."

"Then why don't you come with me?" Jonah cried.

"I will," his mother said. "When I am ready and when I have done my duty by your father. That's what you don't seem to understand. You want everything on your schedule, and that's not how it works. You want Isabella to believe today and me to believe yesterday. And why? Not for us, Jonah. For yourself. You are doing this for yourself and no one else."

"What do you mean?" Jonah felt his face getting hot.

"You think that if someone—anyone—believes, you won't feel as if you've failed. The truth is, you are not using the Lamp to help others to remember Mysterion, but so you can feel worthy."

She stood up, dusting the back of her skirt. She looked down at him.

"You chose truth when you chose the Lamp," she said. "I just spoke the truth. Take it as you wish."

Jonah said nothing.

"I will have lunch waiting, either way," she said.

"I may not be back," Jonah muttered.

"Then I can warm it for dinner."

She picked her way down to the beach, leaping among the rocks like a little girl. Jonah watched her. He wanted to be angry—felt angry—but another side of him realized she was right. After all, what was that impulsive attempt to speak about the Lamp with Isabella, except desperation?

Looking at the Lamp, he thought, *Why even bother?* His other voice answered, *Because you were given this task.*

Taking a deep breath in, Jonah picked up the Lamp. It felt heavier than ever as he rested it on his knees. With a sense of doing what he had done so many times before, he blew gently into the Lamp's core.

CHAPTER TWENTY-THREE

JONAH OPENS HIS EYES

zrel descended through the mist-bank to where the New Elder and Sartish waited in the tossing skiff.

"She went over," the Angelus called softly.

Sartish shook his head in disbelief.

"She did," Azrel said. "I witnessed it."

"And you will remember?" the New Elder said.

"I wouldn't give this away to anyone," Azrel replied. "This is mine."

"You see," the New Elder told Sartish.

Sartish shrugged. "She won't be back."

"She will," the New Elder said. "I will sleep now and go down to her, and in time she will come back. Azrel, take us to the nearest safe harbor. When I awake in the morning, we will return to my island. The others are waiting for us to return and deliver them from the pirate siege."

"Yes, Your Highness." Azrel sighed.

As the New Elder settled himself to sleep in the bottom of the skiff, the Angelus gestured at Sartish to toss her the bow-line. He hesitated. She clicked her tongue and descended to pick it up herself.

"I have to say," she declared, "it always amazes me that the Wind would choose such weaklings as the guides of Mysterion!" Radiant and fluttering, she took up the slack of the line on her shoulder. The skiff came around to follow the Angelus west, tossing its bow against the waves.

Curled up in the hull, his eyes half-closed, the New Elder could just make out Sartish's face looking down at him with an expression he could not quite decipher. The New Elder had just begun to wonder whether his friend was going to make it through, when sleep descended upon him.

Then Jonah inhaled with a gasp and opened his eyes.

He was sitting on the rocks above the beach, with the Angeli's Lamp resting on his knees. The sea glittered mutely at him under the sun, and the monsoon breeze carried the cool tinge of salt water to his lips.

As it always did when he opened his eyes, the visual memory of Mysterion hovered in the back of his mind, like the after-image of something he had been staring at, then faded rapidly. Still, its presence was there, like a deep, quiet reservoir flowing beneath his consciousness.

Focusing now on the present, he remembered Isabella and what his mother had recounted—Isabella's running away, Monsieur Morgan being stabbed—but no trace of his former despair remained.

Today will be different, he thought. He could not explain why, but he was certain of it as he was certain of breathing.

He picked up the Lamp and made his way to the takamaka tree, where he concealed it again. Then he leapt down the rocks and strode up the beach towards the sea road and the Morgan property.

CHAPTER TWENTY-FOUR
RETURN TO NOW

She could no longer feel or see her limbs. They had dissolved into the stream around her. Light of this brilliance would have blinded her natural eyes, but she could somehow take it all in. Her mind and vision were everywhere and nowhere at once. Her thoughts were perfectly empty, utterly still at last.

After a time—she could not tell how long—the streams of light around her began to shiver, like waves feeling the shore. Before she could articulate the thought, she was into breaking light, then through.

Now she was flying across an empty ocean. She was still transparent, so that everything—water, air, light—passed through her without resistance. The ocean was green, tossed into great waves and teeming with dragons, strange skeletal fish, and immense creatures with flippers. Clouds piled and crowded overhead, shot through in moments by white sunbeams. As she rushed through curtains of rain and hurricane winds, the clouds vanished and the water turned from green to the dark blue she knew so well. Blue sky now opened above her, broken occasionally as thunderheads burst forth with storms before dissolving as quickly as they had gathered. The sun rose behind her and set before her in endless succession, flashing like a strobe light in her face. Ahead, the horizon was empty, but even as she flew towards it, a thousand million sunsets flickered and peaks of land rose above the water's surface. Swelling as she approached, the islands took on the familiar shape of her homeland. As she looked, trees sprouted and shot upward, growing over the surface of the land like an instant green skin. Waves of birds flocked back and forth overhead. On the shore, lizard-like shapes lay motionless.

A ship appeared ahead of her, bucking in the waves just beyond the reef—a blue-painted dhow with a great white sail. An instant later, the dhow vanished, and three ships rounded the headland: square-rigged ships, frigates. They too vanished, and Bella passed the reef and stepped onto the shore. She slowed to glide up the beach, drifting through scenes painted on the air: a couple sat and watched the ocean; a small boy built a sandcastle; shadowy figures danced by firelight.

The sun set and night came over.

As she floated up through the trees towards the sea road, she saw couples embracing like ghosts in the shadows; two men furtively digging a hole amid the trees, one holding up a smoky lantern.

The sun rose. Light flooded down.

She followed the road now—a wide beaten path where black slaves in chains and loincloths shuffled up to the plantations; mule-drawn carts groaned under their loads of cinnamon bark or coconuts; ladies perpetually cool-looking in the heat strolled with umbrellas and muslin veils over their faces; plantation owners in linen suits smoked pipes in the shade; a priest in a white cassock strode by.

Sunset and sunrise, sunset and sunrise. Days passed, more than she could count.

Bella approached the place where her parents' driveway should be, but it was overgrown with grass and bushes. Perhaps it didn't yet exist. The flickering scenes had changed—the descendants of the slaves now wore tattered clothes and walked with fishing nets or hefted hoes and picks. A well-dressed white couple in an ancient automobile rattled past on the road that was paved now, and the path to her home opened in the vegetation even as she reached it.

A couple strolled ahead of her, entwined together. Bella thought there was something familiar about them, but she was not certain until they stopped in front of her to kiss. Her mother was young and beautiful, and her father's face possessed a gentleness she had never seen. The image overwhelmed her, and then she passed through them like a curtain and they were gone.

She was turning off the path now, along the trail that was freshly beaten at first, but aged and became overgrown with vegetation even as she followed it. The growth posed no obstacle for her, however: she drifted through and up, finding her way unerringly, driven forward by the same stream that had carried her before—Okean now flowing invisibly beneath the surface of Lethes.

Time was slowing. The sun floated down. The moon rose like a white spotlight seeking her through the trees.

The heart-shaped rock, the bent-old-man tree. Then she was in the moonlit graveyard. Her other self sat against the stone on the far side. A man in a suit squatted with his back to her. Bella drifted among the overgrown headstones, but neither her other self nor the man in the suit noticed.

The moon descended behind her. From the east, light grew and spread like feathers over the dome of the sky.

Before her eyes, the man in the suit swelled into an immense horned creature. With a strange bitterness but without surprise, she knew him as Malach, the Djinn who had brought her to Mysterion. He was holding out something to her other self, and Bella knew what it was even before she saw it—the pendant. The Djinn's lips were moving and as she passed through him, she wanted to reach and rip his tongue out. But her other self was already reaching out for the pendant as the sunlight pierced the trees and touched the dewy grass. Bella Couteau met Isabella Morgan, just as she grabbed the stone that hung from the claws of the Djinn.

* * *

ISABELLA MORGAN OPENED her eyes.

Shafts of sunlight dropped through the trees. In the tangle of grass and bushes, the graveyard headstones shone white and tired. Isabella's eyes rested on them. She felt as if she was waiting to sink down into the earth, to lose herself forever in that silence, slowly overgrown and forgotten, while the headstone at her back would keep watch over her until the end of time.

Somewhere above her hung the visions of her life before this moment: the great falls at the edge of Mysterion; the expanse leading west from the Keepers of the Phoenix and the solitaries who kept silence until the end of Mysterion; the island of Monvieil and the forest of Seeing Pools where her knife arm had failed her. And beyond that, the mermaids spoke into her thoughts, and Qatala and Tala the giant turtle would never see each other, for one would always be absent. At the edge of his one-palm-tree island, Cyclops still floated face down, but she would face that death no more, because now Bella Couteau was running away through the dark trails of Hodoul's island with armfuls of stolen Claw. At night, she slept under the mangrove tree at the edge of the parlay square or wandered restlessly like a stray cat through the broken-down shacks. And when the loneliness bit too hard, she climbed through Disagree's windows and curled up on the mattress he had set out for just that purpose.

At the far edge of her mind stood that unmarked island swathed in smoke and fire and the Nightmare Tree where she had been cast only moments after grasping Malach's pendant; moments so long ago.

And yet it was just a moment ago . . . Yes, she thought. *It happened just now . . .*

As if a tide had turned inside her, the memories of Mysterion began to ebb, first becoming blurred, then distant, like an image flowing backward in time. She reached out to grasp at them, but they rushed away from her in silence, growing more swiftly distant even as the scene before her—gravestones lit by morning sunlight and almost overgrown by vegetation—hardened until at last it was simply the impervious surface of reality, the moment spread before her.

The trees at the far side of the clearing rustled, and a boy emerged. She recognized him at once, but did not wave or call out. He stared at her and started across the cemetery, picking his way around the headstones, but occasionally tripping on one concealed in the grass. He tangled briefly in the out-flung branches of a thorn bush. Then he was beside her, squatting.

Neither of them spoke. In the top of a tree, a go-away bird began to sing. The heat of the day strengthened, turning the air the consistency of warm oil. The gravestone faces glowed under the sun.

"I thought I'd find you here," Jonah said.

"Did you tell my parents?"

"Of course not."

Isabella shrugged. "I don't know."

"Well," Jonah said. "You should. By now."

"Did they call the police?"

"No. They were talking about your aunt though."

"Which aunt?"

"The one who lives on Praslin."

Isabella made a face. "Sending me to her, you mean?"

Jonah rocked his head. "They were talking about it."

"They wouldn't have the guts."

"Well." Jonah shrugged. "It's one way out. Better than this all the time."

"All right," Isabella said. "You can stop laying it on."

She stood and dusted off her pants. "I need a smoke. You want to come with me?"

Jonah looked tired, but nodded. "Okay."

For a moment, Isabella looked down at the headstone. She had read it countless times, but now, something stirred as she glanced at the familiar words—a shape of someone she had known, which had faded with the dream of that place whose name she could no longer quite recall.

"Did you ever have the feeling," she said, "that you were someone else, watching yourself do things?"

Jonah's eyes were compassionate. "You mean—as if you were inside someone else's head."

"Yes." She nodded emphatically. "Exactly."

"Yes," Jonah said. "I did."

"What did you do?"

He could just detect the pleading in her voice. "One day I woke up and found it was all a dream."

Isabella was silent. Finally, she said, "Let's go."

They began to pick their way across the cemetery, Jonah walking ahead of her.

"One thing," he said as they went. "Before we get your smokes, can we make a little detour? There's something I want to show you." He spoke softly, as if the words might somehow damage her.

"What is it?" she asked.

Jonah did not look around. His voice was still quiet. "You'll see."

"Mysterious!" Isabella exclaimed.

Jonah flashed a brief smile back at her. "In a way."

Isabella was aware of the trees shrieking with birds, the weight of the sunlight, the silent depths of the earth beneath her. Everything now seemed to conceal something else, everything somewhere else. In that moment, she finally allowed some great weight to collapse upon her. And instead of being crushed, she found herself buoyed upward in a tide of lightness.

"Yes," she said. "All right." The memory she had glimpsed looking down at the headstone now resurfaced, sharpened into a more definite form: a man with skin like lava from an ancient volcano, a bald head like a beacon, and . . . Glancing back at the headstone, she murmured, "His ancestor was a slave."

"What's that?" Jonah said.

"Nothing," she replied. "I just remembered someone. Keep going."

She broke into a jog to catch up with Jonah, as he flashed a smile back at her. Together, they reached the edge of the cemetery and entered the trees, heading back down the hill towards the sea road.

Deserted, the clearing fell once again into the quiet of the dead, a quiet somehow heightened by the racket of birds squabbling for fruit high in the trees. The sun arched overhead, baking the headstones before descending into the tree line where Jonah and Isabella had gone. Just before it did so, however, a few of its rays touched the east side of the clearing and the face of Isabella's favorite headstone. The rays, tinged golden by dust, played idly on the stone's surface, underscoring the worn and fading etching of the inscription carved in hasty letters:

JEAN DESAGRY. DIED 1802

GLOSSARY

p. 10   NYS—National Youth Service, a required period of service for all children 15 years of age or older.

p. 14   *Calou*—An alcoholic brew made from fermented coconuts.

p. 15   *Mon pauvre*—"My poor one"

p. 44   "In irons"—When a sailing vessel is pointed directly at the wind and cannot easily turn away.

p. 103   *Couyon*—"Fool"

p. 115   *La daube*—A dessert made of sweet potatoes or breadfruits boiled in coconut milk and sugar.

p. 115   *Sous le montaigne*—"Up the mountain"

p. 129   *Tec-tec* soup—A soup made of tiny clams.

p. 130   *Avec son frères*—"With their companions"

p. 149   *Marmite*—A small charcoal barbecue

p. 158   *Karung*—A type of fish

p. 187   *Kaf*—A derogatory and insulting term for someone of African origin.

ACKNOWLEDGMENTS

FOR THE CREATION and publication of this work, I would like to extend my thanks to a number of people. First and foremost, I am grateful as always to my beautiful wife Jaime, for her untiring support and confidence when everything was unclear. I am grateful to Kristi Boyko, a young student whose educational challenges inspired me to write this book in the first place. A big thanks to the staff of Coteau Books, who were so kind, patient and professional in their dealings with me, and for Conciliar Press, for taking me in without hesitation.

ABOUT THE AUTHOR

AS A BOY GROWING UP in the Seychelles, Kenya, Zimbabwe, and Tanzania, Richard René experienced the rich mixture of peoples, myths, and cultures which now finds a place in his fiction. Richard lives with his wife Jaime and three children in Cranbrook, British Columbia, where he is the priest of Saint Aidan Orthodox Mission (www.saintaidan.ca).

Conciliar Media Ministries hopes you have enjoyed and benefited from this book. The proceeds from the sales of our books only partially cover the costs of operating our nonprofit ministry—which includes both the work of Conciliar Press and the work of Ancient Faith Radio. Your financial support makes it possible to continue this ministry both in print and online. Donations are tax-deductible and can be made at www.ancientfaith.com.

ANCIENT FAITH RADIO

Internet Based Orthodox Radio:
Podcasts, 24 hour music and talk stations,
teaching, conference recordings, and much more,
at www.ancientfaith.com